Phone sex? Sophia thought wildly

She had only been teasing Mitch but now she didn't know where to begin. In the past, Mitch had always taken charge in the bedroom. "Are you naked?" she finally ventured, clutching the receiver.

"Just about. I'm wearing a pair of jeans. You?"

"Just a T-shirt," she said. One that had belonged to Mitch but she couldn't bear to throw out.

"What are you wearing underneath it?" he asked, his voice clearly on edge.

"Nothing."

He groaned. "Babe, you're killing me."

"Good," she said, laughing. "Take off your jeans and climb on the bed."

"Only if you do the same." A moment later her breathing grew deeper. "Sophia?"

"I'm there with you, straddling your hips. You're so hard..."

"Harder than ever before," he agreed. "And you're so wet...."

Sophia moaned and lay back on the pillows. She heard Mitch panting on the other end of the phone. She wished she were in bed with him right now. Wished she could feel his heat surrounding her...that she was no longer alone.

Dear Reader,

I'm so excited about *One Hot Weekend*. Though this is my first book for the Harlequin Blaze line, I've written several Silhouette Desire books. I love romance and the feeling that comes with falling in love.

Mitch Hollaran is a man with a mission, and that mission is revenge. He's spent the last ten years rebuilding his career and trying to forget the woman who betrayed him—Sophia Deltonio.

Sophia has carefully hidden her passionate nature behind a winning career as an Assistant District Attorney—until Mitch sends her a reminder of their past steamy relationship. She soon recognizes this is the opening move in a very dangerous game of forbidden desire.

I hope you enjoy reading *One Hot Weekend* as much as I enjoyed writing it!

Katherine Garbera

Books by Katherine Garbera

SILHOUETTE DESIRE

Don't miss any of our special offers. Write to us at the following address for information on our newest releases.

Harlequin Reader Service
U.S.: 3010 Walden Ave., P.O. Box 1325, Buffalo, NY 14269
Canadian: P.O. Box 609, Fort Erie, Ont. L2A 5X3

ONE HOT WEEKEND

Katherine Garbera

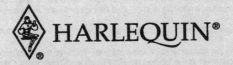

HARLEQUIN®

TORONTO • NEW YORK • LONDON
AMSTERDAM • PARIS • SYDNEY • HAMBURG
STOCKHOLM • ATHENS • TOKYO • MILAN • MADRID
PRAGUE • WARSAW • BUDAPEST • AUCKLAND

For Matt, who is always my hero

Acknowledgments:

There are so many people to thank. My trail to Blaze was a long one and along the way I had a lot of helping hands—first Birgit Davis-Todd, who took some time at the beginning to talk to me about Blaze and what the line was going to be. Julie Leto, who took time on the phone with me and offered some sound advice. Tony and Lori Karayianni, who gave a nudge when I was ready to give up on Blaze. Brenda Chin, who brainstormed ideas with me. And when I finally had an idea that would work for Blaze, I wasn't sure I could do it. Thanks especially to Eve Gaddy, who told me to stop whining and write the book!

ISBN 0-373-79128-3

ONE HOT WEEKEND

Copyright © 2004 by Katherine Garbera.

Visit us at www.eHarlequin.com

Printed in U.S.A.

1

SOPHIA DELTONIO WAS at the top of her game. And everyone knew it. As she strode down the long hall-way past the offices of the other assistant District Attorneys in Orange County, Florida, they all looked up and smiled at her. She'd just won a very difficult case, one she knew would impress Joan Mueller, her boss.

She paused in front of the door with the brass nameplate. Sophia Deltonio, Assistant District Attorney. If she played her cards right, it would read Deputy District Attorney in a short while. She then opened the door to her outer office.

"Hey, boss lady. Great job in court," her secretary Alice said.

"Thanks." She took the messages Alice handed her and entered her office. On the credenza were an assortment of balloons, flowers and a prank gift basket of condoms and crotchless panties from the other ADAs.

She'd just finished prosecuting the panty-raider, as he liked to be called. He'd stolen over one hundred thousand dollars in lacy underwear and sex aids from a local adults-only store. The things she did to keep the world safe from crime, she thought with a wry smile.

In the middle of her desk was another basket, which stopped her cold. It wasn't exactly a basket but a small faux metal washtub. It was wrapped in cellophane and tied with a black velvet ribbon. The ribbon set off a chain reaction inside her.

A lifetime ago, she'd worn a ribbon like that around her neck every day. *It's just a coincidence.* She dropped her briefcase and moved closer to her desk.

There was a card taped to the cellophane and she could see a ring of Corona beer bottles inside there. *Oh, this wasn't good.*

She never drank anything but Pinot Grigio anymore. She almost didn't want to open the card but that was foolish. It was just a card. It had no power over her.

As she studied the cream-colored envelope, a shiver of anticipation moved down her spine. Her hand shook but not from fear. A tingling awareness rippled through her.

This is so stupid. I'm thirty-two for chrissakes and in control of my life.

The handwriting wasn't familiar to her. Of course, it wouldn't be familiar. "Stop being ridiculous."

Mitch Hollaran had been out of her life for a long time and he wasn't suddenly going to show up again. She used her French-manicured nail to open the back of the envelope, and pulled out a card. Instead of the standard FTD one, the thick vellum bore the monogram of a prestigious Los Angeles law firm.

Her stomach sank. She opened the card and inside was the handwriting she recognized—bold, brash and filled with the kind of passion a girl could die from knowing.

See you in court.

There was no signature, just a scrawled *M*. But then she didn't need a signature to know it was from Mitch. She sank down on one of the guest chairs and closed her eyes.

Memories of the man she once knew and of the passion they'd shared assailed her. The Corona incident had happened right before they'd broken up. Too poor to be able to afford a winter vacation, they'd stayed in their apartment near the Harvard campus where they both were studying law, with the thermostat cranked up to eighty, listening to blues music and making love for four days.

She seldom let herself think about that life. She was a different woman now. She was in line to become the Deputy D.A. in Orange County. All of

Orlando knew she was a woman to be reckoned with inside the courtroom and out.

And she no longer indulged the sensual side of her personality. She'd learned the hard way that professional drive and personal passion didn't mix inside her. They might for other women, but not for her.

She hadn't had a lover since Robert had left her eighteen months earlier. He'd wanted marriage and Sophia hadn't been able to commit herself to him. She hadn't analyzed it and didn't want to. She just knew Robert wasn't as important as her career and never would be.

That's probably why Mitch's reappearance in her life was making her hot inside by dredging up memories of the most erotic time in her life.

But instead of focusing on that, she reached for the tin and pulled open the cellophane. Inside were six Coronas and a bag of limes. Next to the limes was a Stevie Ray Vaughan CD. She shivered hearing the raspy sound of Vaughan's blues in her head and remembering Mitch's fingers on her neck. Cool and wet with the juice of the lime, stroking down her back.

Her phone rang and she jumped. She put a hand to her neck and took a deep breath before answering the call.

"This is Deltonio."

"Joan wants to see you in her office," Alice said.

"Now?"

"As soon as you can make it. It involves the Spinder case."

"Thanks, Alice. Tell her I'll be right down."

Sophia hung up the phone. She slipped the note and black velvet ribbon from Mitch into her briefcase. She took the Corona bucket and put it on the credenza behind the panty basket. Though hidden from view, the washtub continued to taunt her with memories.

The blues riffs of Stevie's guitar echoed through her mind as she remembered the thrill of Mitch's touch. *This wasn't good.*

She had to focus. The Spinder case involved a Hollywood hotshot and a seventeen-year-old girl, Holly McBride. The charge against Jason Spinder was having sex with a minor. The alleged act had taken place last fall when Holly was only sixteen. Jason had been shooting his latest blockbuster—this summer's *Maximum Exposure* in Orlando.

Sophia ran the facts of the case through her head, pushing Mitch back into the past. She was meeting with her boss and couldn't—wouldn't—let a man from her past interfere with her career. Damn. She needed a date a hell of a lot more than she'd thought if one basket could whip her into a frenzy like this.

She took a tube of Bobbi Brown lipstick from her

purse and carefully touched up her lips. She fluffed her shoulder-length hair, then smoothed it into place. She banished Stevie Ray Vaughan from her mind and instead focused on ACDC's "Back In Black." The song she always played before entering the courtroom. The raucous rock 'n' roll never failed to pump up her blood and make her feel invincible.

She grabbed the file and notes she'd made on the Spinder case. Already the D.A.'s office had more press than normal and she wasn't looking forward to the media circus a high-profile defendant would bring.

That explained the basket of Coronas. From the news clippings and alumni newsletters she'd scanned guiltily for news about Mitch, she knew he'd developed a reputation for winning that anyone would envy. In fact, he was fast becoming the pre-eminent lawyer to the stars. Mitch had to be Spinder's lawyer.

Of course, he'd have to reenter her life now when things were finally on track. When she wasn't scraping to make a career and she'd finally found a place where she was comfortable being alone.

Damn, after ten years it shouldn't matter that he was coming back. Except she knew it wasn't going to be a happy reunion. She knew that she'd done him wrong in the worst way a woman could. She knew that he hadn't forgotten or forgiven her. The

Coronas and the CD guaranteed he was coming out here for more than courtroom victory.

He was coming for revenge.

JOAN MUELLER WATCHED her protégé nervously chew on her lower lip. Sophia usually brimmed with energy—ready to take on any challenge. But there was something different about her today.

"What took you so long to get here?" Joan asked. It had been fifteen minutes since her initial call. It wasn't the first time that Sophia had taken her time arriving so that didn't bother her. But there was something off about Sophia today.

"I had to find the file," Sophia said.

That made sense. Sophia was the most organized attorney she had on staff and also the busiest. "Congratulations on your win."

"Thanks. I can safely say that prosecuting a man called the panty-raider is something I never expected to do."

"That's what I love about this office. We see some really different cases."

"That's one way to put it," Sophia said.

"Are you ready for this afternoon?" Normally, she wouldn't have mentioned the arraignment phase of the case but with all the press interest she wanted to make sure every detail was smooth as silk.

"Um…about that. My caseload is really heavy. I was wondering if…?"

Joan sat back in her chair. Where was Sophia going with this? Sophia needed a high-profile win to add to her already impressive résumé to make her a definite shoo-in for the Deputy position. Joan had mentored the younger woman since she'd come on staff nearly seven years ago.

"Sophia, what's wrong? You're the only one I considered for this case. You need the practice with the press." She'd been grooming Sophia for the Deputy D.A. position and until this moment hadn't had any doubts that Sophia was the right attorney for the job.

She mentally went through the other candidates. Joseph O'Neill was a possibility. He was young and hungry. But Joan had wanted to see another woman succeed her when she retired.

"You're right," Sophia said.

"When this case is over you can take some time off," Joan said. Sophia hadn't taken a vacation since starting with the D.A.'s office. She'd never wanted one before.

"I do need a vacation," Sophia admitted.

This case was important to the District Attorney's office because it was high-profile.

Joan remembered her fifth year in the office and the decisions she'd had to make. At that time Maurice Hanner was still asking her out. And after a brief affair she'd thought about marrying him. But in the end no man could hold a candle to the law for her.

She hoped Sophia made the same choice. But just in case, Joan decided to start keeping a closer eye on Joseph.

REVENGE WAS BEST SERVED cold, Mitch Hollaran had heard. He didn't care what temperature it was now that the end was in sight. For ten years he'd lived by a vow he'd made as a young man of twenty-four. When he'd followed his gonads instead of his head and had his ass served to him by a black-haired witch who still haunted his dreams.

He'd like to think he was a smarter man at thirty-four but there were days when he doubted it. Today wasn't one of them. Everything was going his way. His flight had landed early. The exotic rental car service had a black Porsche waiting for him. He'd gotten a call from his office that the package he'd ordered had been delivered to Sophia.

He'd have loved to see Sophia's face when she'd received his calling card, letting her know he was back in town. And back in her life.

Just the thought of seeing Sophia Deltonio again was enough to make him hard. It wasn't just that she'd put him in an untenable position with the law firm he'd hoped to work for. It was that she'd ravaged his nice, neat plans for the future.

All of the Hollaran men had married their college sweethearts. Four generations of men had set the expectation for Mitch that women met in that phase of life were the ones to make a family with. Sophia had embodied everything he'd wanted in a woman and then she'd ripped that image to shreds with one coldly calculated move.

Though he was content with his life, he wouldn't rest until he came out of an encounter with her the winner. And to think he was going to have to thank his pain-in-the-ass client Jason Spinder for the pleasure.

Mitch had talked with Spinder on the phone before leaving L.A. The case was basically one of "he said," "she said." Jason claimed that Holly McBride had told him she was eighteen and that others had corroborated her story. But the fact of the matter was Jason did have sex with Holly and she was underage. It was Mitch's job to prove to the jury that Holly had tricked Jason for her own gain, using her body to get what she wanted.

Since the moment his assistant had sent him the file on Jason and the D.A. who was prosecuting the case Mitch had thought of nothing but the woman who'd betrayed him.

He had a chance to go up against the one woman

he'd lost against so long ago. And this time he intended to come out the winner.

He'd had other lovers since they parted but he'd never let one woman consume him the way he'd let Sophia that long-ago winter. He'd been young.

Hell, he'd been a damned sap. But not anymore. He knew she had to have changed as well. And he needed to see the woman she was today. To exorcise the woman she was out of his system and move on.

In his mind he always pictured her wearing the velvet ribbon choker and nothing but lime juice. He swallowed and shifted his legs. She'd been one hell of a lover and the most sensual lady he'd ever met.

Everything with her had been erotic. Even law. He shook his head. He adjusted the radio dial off the pop station to some boisterous country music. It seemed to suit Orlando. The city was big and sophisticated but still clung to its cow-town roots. He maneuvered his way through the traffic thinking about Sophia.

She possessed hidden depths that she'd reveal to no man. Or at least she'd never revealed them to him. Years ago, he'd been planting the seeds for the future with her. But she'd wanted him only for what he could give her in bed. Well, that was fine; he no longer cared about the secrets of her soul.

He'd kept track of her through the alumni newsletter and the articles she'd written for the Harvard

Law Bulletin. He'd seen a picture of her about a year ago when she'd won a humanitarian award.

It had ruined the coldhearted bitch image he had of her but he knew that it was pride that had made him think of her in those terms. Because truth be told if he'd had the same information she'd had, he wasn't too sure he wouldn't have sent her down a false trail and then claimed the one spot in the prestigious law firm, just as she had done to him.

He'd returned to Los Angeles and finished his graduate work at UCLA's Law School. Fueled by the need to prove his worth to Sophia and the firm that had not selected him, he had scored a position in a very prestigious firm in Los Angeles and had recently been named an associate of the firm.

He knew that a gentleman would let the past rest. His father had counseled him many times to let go of things. But then Peter Hollaran had married his high-school sweetheart and had gone to work in his dad's hardware store. His dad's life was a bit simpler than Mitch's.

Mitch had never been able to forget past wrongs. It was one of his faults and he'd made peace with a majority of his mistakes, but not Sophia. She haunted his dreams from time to time. And he knew it was time to force her out of his system once and for all.

Everything seemed to be coming together at once.

He was on his own again since he'd refused to marry his live-in lover and she'd left him. He was finally facing the one woman who had left him hanging. He was plotting the kind of revenge that made him feel a little slimy, but then betrayal was something he knew Sophia understood.

So he didn't really feel that bad. He didn't regret the path his life had taken. He was a successful man by anyone's standards, but deep inside the fire that had been driving him toward success was fueled by a deep-seated need for retribution.

He downshifted the Porsche Turbo and pulled into the downtown courthouse parking lot.

Who would have thought Jason Spinder, the twenty-two-year-old action movie star, would be the one to deliver it to him? Mitch entered the courthouse and spotted Jason standing off to one side with his manager, Marcus Richardson. Both men nodded at Mitch as he entered. He went through the metal detector and joined them.

"Hollaran, I thought you weren't going to make it," Jason said. Jason wasn't overly attractive by Hollywood standards. But he had charisma, according to Betsy, Mitch's secretary.

"Of course I made it. That's what you pay me for."

"What's going to happen today?" Jason asked. He didn't look like a blockbuster action star who commanded ten million dollars a picture. Instead he looked like a young kid in over his head.

"You're going to be arraigned."

"Then?"

"Wait for the trial to be set."

"Oh, God. This is such a mess. Marcus has been trying to put a positive spin on it. But I think this is going to hurt my chances for an Oscar this year."

"Let Marcus handle the media, that's what he does best. I'll handle the judge and jury. You just relax."

"I can't, man. My career is on the line and I don't want to be blackballed because of this."

"This is going to be tricky, Jason. I won't lie to you, but I don't intend to lose this case."

"I heard the D.A.'s office is sending their barracuda," Jason said.

"I'm a licensed fisherman."

Jason cracked a smile. Then the three men headed down the hall toward the courtroom where Jason was scheduled to appear. Mitch stopped at the water fountain for a drink. "I'll catch up with you inside."

Mitch needed a few minutes to himself to prepare to see Sophia again. Perhaps the years hadn't been kind to her. With more than a little spite, he imagined her overweight and graying.

With that image firmly in mind, he started for the courtroom ready to meet his nemesis. The door opened as he approached it and a woman barreled out with her head down and ran straight into Mitch.

He steadied her and then looked down into eyes he'd never forgotten. They were wide and a deeper blue than the Pacific Ocean at sunset. He started to release her, then stopped.

Her hips were a remembered softness under his flexed fingers. She shifted in his embrace, then seemed to realize what she was doing and tried to push away. He kept her close.

She held herself stiffly in his arms and he liked knowing he'd thrown her off guard.

"Mitch," she said.

Just his name, but the tone of her voice stroked over his skin like a velvet glove bringing each nerve to quivering attention. He realized suddenly that revenge did have a temperature and it had just gotten much hotter.

2

SOPHIA CLOSED HER EYES and for a minute was tempted to put her arms around Mitch. Dammit, she was over him. Way over him. She'd made her choice and she'd been happily living with it. Until now. Until she'd felt his strong arms around her once again. He wasn't doing anything improper but she remembered every time he had.

Her stomach sank to her toes. She pumped up her internal background music. "Back in Black" was blaring inside her head louder than in a teenage metal-head's room. She stepped away from him as soon as her feet were steady.

But not far enough. She doubted if Miami would be far enough to blunt the impact of seeing him in the flesh again. The Coronas had swirled to life memories of a different time and a different person. But she felt as though she'd successfully relegated that woman to the past until this moment.

Face-to-face with the one man she'd never really forgotten, she tried to blunt the sensations spreading throughout her body. As one of Mitch's hands swept upward, lingering on that spot on the base of her neck, she realized he hadn't forgotten her either.

AC/DC died an abrupt end inside her head.

Everything feminine in her sprang to attention and the sensual sounds of Stevie Ray Vaughan started playing in her mind. Her breasts felt full and heavy, her nipples tingled. His body heat shimmered between them. Damn, only an inch of space separated them. If she leaned forward she'd be pressed against the hard planes of his chest.

Each breath he took brushed across her face. He smelled of peppermint gum. The first time they'd kissed he'd been chewing peppermint. The taste had infused her mouth.

She recognized the signs of arousal in him. His pupils were dilated, his nostrils flared with his exhalation. While she appreciated the fact the awareness wasn't all one-sided, they still had to try a case against each other. She had to be on her toes and functioning like the cool, calm Assistant D.A. she was. Not some hormone-driven woman.

When she'd been twenty-two and in the throes of her love affair with him she'd indulged her sensual side with no thought of the consequences. Now that she was in her thirties, she thought she'd banked those fires but everything about Mitch, from his dark hair to his cold gray eyes was stirring up the embers.

Shivering a little she stepped away. Mitch made

her want to do something unpredictable like caress his face and kiss his full lips. Would he still taste the same? Taste him and find out, her traitorous body cried out.

But her mind had finally wakened and bellowed for her to get out of there. She'd been on her way to the bathroom for her pretrial ritual pep talk.

Focus on the job. Mitch was just like any other defense attorney, except he smelled better.

"Thanks for catching me," she said, and walked toward the ladies' bathroom. It was only twenty paces to the washroom. Counting the steps was part of her ritual.

She'd taken five of them when he moved. Her senses were still attuned to him. He was following her. Her first instinct was to walk faster and get away from him.

But she'd never been a coward. So instead she slowed her steps, letting her hips sway with each one. She knew he was watching her.

"Sophia?"

She glanced over her shoulder at him. He'd noticed. His gaze was on her backside. She hid her smile. The girl still had it, she thought. She was glad to know she wasn't alone in this ill-timed attraction. "Yes."

"This isn't finished."

Immediately her internal victory turned to defeat.

This was a new Mitch, a stranger with a familiar face. She wasn't sure how to deal with him. "Is that a threat, Mitch?"

He closed the gap between them. He slid one hand down her back, cupping her butt and said, "Hell, no. That's a promise, baby. And you know I always keep my promises."

He turned toward the courtroom. She should let him go but she didn't like him having the last word or touching her in that blatantly masculine way. She pivoted quickly, taking his hand and pulling him down the hall into a little alcove between the courtrooms.

He raised one eyebrow at her and she scowled at him. In her mind she fixed an image of herself as a sophisticated winning attorney. But it evaporated, leaving instead a picture of herself with an open bottle of Corona.

"What do you want from me?" she asked.

He shrugged. "I'm not sure."

"That doesn't sound like you. You always know what you want."

"I learned not to share my desires with just anyone, baby."

His words hurt. They were justified but still she hadn't expected them to. "Would it help if I said I was sorry?"

"I don't know, are you?"

She couldn't answer him. She wanted to say yes. But she knew she wouldn't be the woman she was today if she'd acted differently ten years ago. She regretted hurting him. But at the time she hadn't seen any other way. Mitch had always made her feel things too intensely.

The false trail she'd sent him on had been designed to give her the upper hand and it had. Because Mitch had spent time researching her lead— giving her the real advantage in the tough race they'd both been running.

She did know that other than that one time she'd never lied to him. And she hadn't lied since. Not even social white lies. She been burned by that incident, and moving on had left her a different woman. "I'm not sure."

In his eyes she thought she saw a bit of the compassionate young man he'd once been. The man who'd always understood her drive to succeed and be the best. "I know."

"Can we come to some kind of truce?" she said at last.

"No," he replied, quickly.

She nodded. "I'm not asking you to give up your feelings of resentment toward me. I'm just asking for a temporary hold."

"I'm listening."

"I don't have it all worked out yet. Can we talk about this in my office after we're done in court?"

"Okay. We can share the beer I sent you."

"Oh, did you send me something?" she asked, patting his ass and walking away from him.

"You know I did, baby," he growled as he walked past her into the courtroom.

She watched him go, wondering what it was going to take to satisfy Mitch and the rekindled desire burning in the center of her body. She tried to tell herself he was just another attorney as she stepped into the courtroom but those words rang hollow. No other attorney had ever made her pulse race the way Mitch did.

MITCH LOOSENED HIS TIE and stepped out into the Orlando summer day. It was still hot as hell. He'd talked to the press on the steps of the courthouse. Jason's movie career was hanging in the balance, and he and Marcus both agreed the less their client said the better.

Mitch rolled his shoulders and took his sunglasses from his pocket. Sophia had developed into a hell of a sophisticated woman since he'd last seen her. He wouldn't have expected the girl who'd worn poet shirts and jeans to ever be comfortable in a designer suit.

He got in the Porsche and drove to the D.A.'s

office. He knew he wanted his pound of flesh from the moment he'd stepped on the plane in L.A. His cold-blooded plan for revenge was going to take some careful handling. He'd conveniently forgotten a few important details about her.

The softer things. Despite the fact that she'd sent him on a false trail so she could get the only remaining internship with an important law firm, Sophia had always been very soft.

And when he'd held her in his arms earlier, he'd realized she still was. That softness didn't matter. She was a grown woman and she'd started a very dangerous game with him a lifetime ago.

His phone rang. "Hollaran."

"Mitch, buddy, I got a problem."

Devlin Chase. He closed his eyes and groaned. Devlin was one of his oldest friends. They'd grown up together in the same middle-class *Growing Pains*-style family. Only Dev's parents had gotten a divorce and Dev had never stopped rebelling.

"I'm in Florida. Can this be done over the phone?"

There was a loud sigh. "No."

He heard sounds he hoped weren't familiar. "Are you in jail?"

"Uh…yes."

"What's the charge?"

"Drug possession."

Devlin had checked himself into detox about nine months ago when he'd met a pretty horse trainer who had a zero-tolerance policy for drug users. And Mitch had watched his friend struggle every day but they'd met for drinks a few weeks ago and Devlin had seemed okay. Better than okay, actually more like he finally had gotten his life on track. "I thought you'd cleaned up."

"Shit happens, man."

"Shit only happens to those who let it happen."

"We can't all be the golden boy." Dev was angry. But he had been for the last fifteen years.

"Is that what this is all about?" Mitch asked.

"Hell, no. It's never been about you."

"Hold on. I'm driving."

Mitch pulled onto the shoulder. Dev's timing as usual sucked. He wasn't going to be able to concentrate on manipulating Sophia while worrying about his friend.

Revenge would have to wait. Taking care of his friend was more important. But maybe that was the problem. Mitch was always bailing Dev out. Maybe it was time for some tough love. But Mitch didn't know if he could leave Dev in a cell. Even if that were the best thing for him.

"Give me the details. I'll handle what I can from here. I'm going to have to get someone from my office over there."

He turned off the car and rolled down his window. It was a hot day, reminding Mitch of the summer before junior high school when he and Dev had ruled the neighborhood. They'd been an unstoppable team that year. College had changed them. Mitch had learned that looks and charm weren't enough to make it in the world, but Dev had never made that adjustment.

Taking a notepad he started asking questions. Dev answered them all with the same honesty he'd always had toward his addiction. "I don't think detox is going to work this time."

"You broke your probation."

"Am I going to jail this time?"

"Let me see what I can do. I'll have to call the judge and get bail set. Do you have anyone who can post it?"

"No."

"What about Julie?" Dev was a professional horse breeder and had been working for the last six months with Julie Cavanaugh. And spending most of his nights at her home.

"Don't send Julie."

"Why not?" Mitch wished he were in L.A. so he could check out Dev himself. He didn't know Julie, other than through Dev's stories. But if the woman was half as crazy about Dev as Dev was about her, then she'd want to know.

"She doesn't know I'm an addict."

"Why the hell not?"

"She's kind of classy."

"So?"

"She thinks I'm one of the good guys, man. I don't want her to know I'm not."

Mitch sighed. He, more than anyone else, understood how a woman could mess with a guy's head. "I'll do my best."

He glanced at his watch. He couldn't drive and make the kind of calls he needed to make to take care of Dev's problems.

He called Sophia's office. Her secretary answered on the third ring and put him through.

"Deltonio." Sophia's voice had been hard and very confident in the courtroom. In her office though she sounded like the woman he remembered— sweet, tender and very ladylike. He warned himself not to get drawn into the same trap he had before.

"Hey, babe, its Mitch."

"Mitch, it's the twenty-first century. Most women don't like to be called babe."

"That's not what they tell me," he said.

She sighed and he heard her office chair creak. What was her office like? His corner office in L.A. overlooked the city, and on a smog-free day you could see all the way to the mountains. Did she still have that Monet print of Argenteuil?

"Where are you?"

"In my car. Listen, something's come up in L.A. Can we meet for drinks instead?"

"I don't know," she hedged.

"You're the one who wanted to meet." He thought he heard the Stevie Ray Vaughan playing in the background. He hadn't had a chance to ask her about the gift. Really ask her about it and watch her reactions when she talked about the CD and Coronas. His plan, which was rough, had been to simply torment her with images from their past. Unfortunately that was backfiring on him. The images that he knew would ignite passion within her were having the same result on him.

He heard her shuffling something in the background. "Fine. Where are you staying?"

"At the Westin Grand Bohemian Hotel."

"I'll meet you in the Bösendorfer Lounge. What time?" She was all business now.

"In about an hour or so."

"Good, well, 'bye."

"Sophia?" he asked, pitching his voice lower. He watched for a break in traffic and pulled back onto the highway.

"Yeah."

"Have you been listening to 'Shake For Me'?" he asked.

The music in the background was abruptly silenced. And he knew she had been. "Why would I be?"

"I thought I heard it in the background," he said. That song had been playing when he'd picked her up for their first date. The music had marked a number of firsts for them. They'd blared it from the speakers when they'd moved in together. And it had played in the background when Sophia had done that striptease for him that had made him ravenous for her.

Even now when he heard it on the radio the song had the power to make him hard with the images of Sophia's full curves gyrating around him.

"I...I'm not that woman anymore, Mitch."

"What do you mean by that?"

"Nothing. We'll talk later. I've got to go."

She hung up and he drove to his hotel. He didn't like the way Sophia had sounded before she hung up the phone. He'd always been a protector. That's why he'd chosen law as a profession. He knew weak people made stupid choices and they deserved competent representation.

He was justified in his revenge but hadn't expected tearing her carefully ordered world apart to affect him.

SOPHIA TOOK the opportunity to meet with Joan and reassure her boss that she had everything under control. She knew that she had not been at her best in their meeting earlier this afternoon. Being in court though had reminded her of the importance of her career. And she wasn't going to let Mitch Hollaran derail that.

She set up appointments to speak to Holly McBride and the two girls who'd been in the bar with her when she met Jason Spinder. The alleged sexual act had taken place at a party thrown for the cast and crew of the production. Sophia wanted to interview as many people involved with the case as she could.

But not tonight. Tonight she had to meet with Mitch. Meet with him, talk to him and hopefully put the past to rest so they could both move on. She had to be in court at nine the next morning. Normally she'd be home preparing for the next day. Instead she was in the lobby bar about to meet the one man who was shaking up her life. As much as she resented the time away from work, she had to figure out what Mitch wanted and deal with that.

She took a seat in the piano bar and ordered a glass of wine. She checked her watch. He was already ten minutes late. She'd give him another five and then she was leaving.

She needed to reach some sort of truce with Mitch. If it were only their shared past she'd be able to deal with it. She saw her last lover, Robert, fairly frequently. He was a lower circuit court judge. And they'd become friends of a sort.

But Mitch wasn't a friend. Even if things had ended well between them she knew they'd never be friends because just looking at him made everything womanly in her stand at attention.

The waitress brought her drink. She'd better control this attraction before it destroyed her. If only there were a way to get Mitch out of her system once and for all. The way they'd parted hadn't been satisfying for either of them, and she wondered if this time they both could achieve at least some kind of closure.

"Hey, babe," Mitch said, as he approached her table.

She should have ordered soda water. She needed all of her faculties about her when dealing with Mitch. It wasn't just that he was the embodiment of everything she found sexy in a man. It was that he knew it. His smile said as much and she shivered in reaction.

He still wore the Armani suit he'd had on in court. His tie was neatly tied and he looked as if he'd stepped from the pages of *GQ*. It would have been nice if time had been cruel to him, maybe thinned his hair, given him a beer belly, but if anything he was leaner and harder now than he had been in college.

In comparison she felt unkempt. The air-conditioning in her Mazda was on the fritz and she'd sweated buckets the entire way over. She'd touched up her makeup and hair but she'd been in her suit all day and she wished she was at home wearing a sundress and drinking iced tea on her patio instead of sitting in the crowded lobby of the Westin hotel.

"Mitch," she said, standing to greet him.

He waved her back into her seat and sat down next to her on the padded bench seat instead of in the wing back chair she'd hoped he would take. The cocktail table was close and the lounge made the most of their space, so Mitch was right next to her.

Barely five inches of space separated them. She was painfully aware of her personal space and how close he was to invading it.

He signaled the waitress. "What are you drinking?"

"White wine."

He raised one eyebrow and ordered a Dos Equis. He settled back against the seat and rubbed the bridge of his nose. He looked tired and not at all threatening right now. He didn't seem inclined to talk so she got to the matter at hand.

No matter how vulnerable Mitch Hollaran might seem, his opening move told her he was here for blood. Yet he did look as though he needed a friend.

She wasn't going to ask him what was wrong. She took a sip of her wine.

His beer arrived and he drained half the bottle in one long pull. He stretched his arm along the back of the couch behind her head. His hand rested on her shoulder. He toyed with a strand of her hair.

"Please don't."

"Why not? You used to like it."

She knew she'd been right not to let her guard down around him. "We're not lovers any more."

"That's right. We aren't."

She was surrounded by him. The spicy scent of his cologne, the heat of his body, the weight of his arm. She closed her eyes, but that only intensified her other senses. She opened them and looked straight at the man who was back in her life, and not just because of work.

"What do you want from me, Mitch?" she asked. The sooner she figured it out, the sooner she could escape to her home and rebuild the defenses he'd so easily ripped through.

He tilted her face toward his and the intensity in his eyes set every nerve in her body on fire. Perhaps she should just take him upstairs and have sex with him. Let him be in control of her body, and assuage the ache that was growing as she sat here.

"Everything you have to give," he said.

She clenched her thighs together. She wanted

him. Wanted those big hot hands on her naked body. She wanted to take the Coronas and limes up to his room, put on Stevie Ray and make love to him all night long.

"Why?" she asked.

"Why not?"

"Are we playing a schoolyard game?"

"We're both a little too old for that."

"Then why the word fencing?"

"Honestly, Sophia, you make me feel fourteen again."

"I don't mean to."

"You can't control it. And neither can I. That's why I sent you the basket."

"I don't understand."

"I'm here for more than my client, babe."

He leaned back, drained the rest of his beer. Drawing the tip of one finger down the side of her face, he said, "I'm here to exorcise you from my dreams."

3

MITCH SIGNALED the waitress to bring another beer. Leaning back against the padded seat he observed Sophia. It had taken a lot to fluster her and even now he wasn't quite sure he'd actually done it. Only her tight grip on the stem of her wineglass and the flush on her cheeks gave her true emotions away.

"Wow, I didn't see that coming," she said.

"What did you expect?" he asked.

"I don't know, maybe that you wanted to express some anger."

"Express some anger? If I get pissed off I'm not going to invite you for a drink to 'express myself.'"

"This is the first time we've been alone since college," she said.

"Did that basket lead you to believe I was angry?"

"Not exactly."

He wanted to crack her shell of confidence and lay waste to her dreams the same way she'd shattered his illusions ten years ago. He reached into his pocket and touched the black velvet ribbon he'd kept since they'd parted. The one she'd used to wear at her neck with a little heart pendant he'd given her.

Around them people milled, some going in to dinner, some leaving, and he wished he'd chosen a less public place for this meeting. A place where he could pull her into his arms and see her reaction. Every instinct he possessed insisted he reinstate the physical bond between them, and bind her to him with the pleasures of the flesh.

More than the plans he'd made in the dark were driving him now. The fevered dreams that had haunted him had a chance of becoming reality. He'd been searching for the white-hot passion he'd found in her arms since he'd left her.

Revenge, he reminded himself. But that was no longer his only motivation. The tyrant in his pants was awake now and didn't care that Sophia had betrayed him in the past.

"What did you mean exorcise? In bed?" she asked, tipping her head to the side. One long strand of her thick hair brushed against his hand. Her perfume, a light floral scent, beckoned him closer. He wanted to bury his face in her hair. And then feel it against his naked chest.

Her composure was still shaken but he realized she was slowly pulling it back around her like a cloak. She made him feel too big in the small space.

She seemed so ladylike and gentle that for a moment, he couldn't remember why they were in the bar instead of in his room.

Her nails were pretty and manicured. She tapped one of them on the table. He realized then that simply shocking her wasn't going to be enough to knock her off her guard.

"I don't remember us ever confining ourselves to a bed."

Her lips parted and her eyes widened. He wondered how she'd changed over the years. Her breasts looked a little smaller; he wanted to cup them and find out how much smaller they were. Would her nipples still tighten and nuzzle into his palm, begging for more caresses? She'd always had an extra five pounds that she wanted to lose but the woman before him was slim and very...dainty.

"What makes you think I still want you?"

But he knew she did. He'd seen her reaction in the hallway of the courtroom when he'd stroked the back of her neck. That spot was Sophia's sweetest one. One touch there and she'd turn into a bundle of nerves. Gooseflesh would spread down her body, her nipples would darken and tighten, and she'd get all creamy between her legs. He dropped his hand from the back of the padded bench to her shoulder and she quivered.

"Don't you?" he asked, stroking the side of her

neck with his thumb, making broad circles on her skin, coming closer and closer to that one spot. She inhaled sharply and he decided to toy with her a little more.

He wrapped that long strand of hair around his forefinger. Her hair was a remembered luxury, thick and soft. He ran his hand through that one strand, toying with it. She shuddered and her pupils dilated.

"Stop," she said huskily.

He swallowed. She was soft everywhere. Such a contrast to the hard-as-nails woman he'd seen in court this afternoon. She'd removed her suit jacket and wore only a thin silk shirt. The blouse didn't cling tightly to her breasts but he remembered the shape of her. And he knew he had to have her again.

"I can't. I have to get you out of my system."

She trembled at his words, her mouth parting on a sigh. And he leaned closer to her, brushing her lips with his. Just a light butterfly kiss that promised so much more. She leaned forward as he pulled back.

He licked her bottom lip. Damn, she tasted good. He shifted his grip on her strand of hair until he was instead cupping the back of her head. He didn't want to see her response. Thinking was now beyond him as he ceded control to his instincts.

As he tasted her mouth with long strokes of his tongue, she shifted on the bench, her hands coming to rest on his shoulders. Damn, he wished he'd shed his jacket in his room.

She slipped her hands under the lapels of his jacket as he pressed a lingering kiss to her lips. Her long fingers stroked over his muscles until she found his nipples. She stroked her finger around and around. His cock jumped at the thought of that same caress all over his body.

Thrusting his tongue deeper into her mouth, he moved his hands through her hair. He tasted her as deeply as he could, not stopping until he knew that he'd do something lewd and get them both arrested if he didn't.

He pulled back. Her lips were full and swollen. Her eyes were closed and her nails dug into his pecs. Oh, yeah, they still had it.

That made everything so much easier, yet at the same time more complicated. Because the woman he'd just kissed the socks off of, awakened the man deep inside him that he'd struggled to bury beneath short-term affairs and one-night stands.

She blinked a couple of times and then pushed his hand from her hair.

"What do you want from me?" she asked.

"I already told you."

"Are you only doing this because of the past?"

He looked into those wide blue eyes, and saw the

future and the past converge. And knew that he had to decide how important his revenge on Sophia was.

"I'm not sure anymore."

SOPHIA DIDN'T TOUCH the rest of her wine. She needed a cold glass of water…splashed on her face and overheated body. She'd settle for getting out of the bar fast. Anything to clear her head and shake off the languid feelings he'd evoked.

What she really wanted to do was take his hand and lead him to an empty elevator. Once inside she wanted to hit the emergency close button and finish what that kiss had started while they were secluded and alone. She wanted to make him come so hard that he forgot all his plans about her. Because she saw beyond his arousal to the cold calculation.

But that would be really stupid. Despite her present predicament, Sophia was rarely a victim to her own whims. But her body argued that Mitch was a known quantity and dallying with him wouldn't be stupid and her heart agreed.

Her mind…her mind said if she was going to listen to those two she needed a plan to protect herself. Only a fool would start anything with a man she had once betrayed without planning for the fallout. Because no matter what Mitch felt physically for her, sooner or later the hormones were going to ebb, and he was going to start thinking again and remembering.

"Do you want to talk about the past?" she asked. She kept repeating herself but she was still in a haze of arousal from his kiss.

Ultimately that was why she'd sabotaged Mitch years ago. He'd held a power over her that she doubted he had even known he had. But she'd known. She'd felt it every time they were together and more sharply when they were apart.

Not a day went by that she didn't relive their last moments together and wish she'd been a different woman. One who could have blended both her professional and personal lives and not sacrifice either one.

"Do you?" he asked in that cocky way of his that made her want to smack him.

"Only if it will make you go away," she said. Which was honest. But she hoped he wouldn't go away. Until that basket of beer had landed on her desk she hadn't realized she'd been substituting court wins for real excitement.

He laughed. "Babe, I'm not going anywhere."

Big surprise. This was her penance and semigood Catholic girl that she was, she'd do it. "I was afraid of that."

"Fear can be a good thing."

Their lovemaking had always had an aura of danger around it. Mitch was very dominant and had used that to master her completely. She hadn't minded it in the bedroom, but outside she'd found herself getting lost in the image of what Mitch saw instead of who she really was. "Maybe from where you're sitting."

"The view's very delicious from my seat," he said, eyeing her breasts.

She glanced down and saw that her nipples were plainly visible beneath her silk shirt and lacy bra. Her first impulse was to cross her arms over her chest and hide from him. But hiding wouldn't do any good, so she just thrust back her shoulders and let him look his fill.

"Are you here to ruin my career?" she asked, while he was distracted.

"Babe, don't give yourself too much influence over my actions. I'm here for my client."

That cut her, which wasn't surprising since she'd never really gotten over Mitch. There had been no natural end to their affair. Only that abrupt ending that she'd forced on them. "Why did you send me Corona and Stevie Ray, then?"

"I thought we covered that?" He rubbed the back of his neck and stretched in the too-tight space. Was he a workaholic like her? She hoped not. She hoped he had a balanced life. And she'd always wished that he'd started the family he'd wanted with a nice girl.

"Exorcism?" she asked.

"Yeah."

She thought about what Mitch wanted from her. She was tired of staying home by herself and though self-pleasure worked as a temporary ease, she needed a man. Not just any man but Mitch Hollaran. She needed to find the bridge between the passionate woman she'd once been and the cold one she'd become.

"I've got a deal for you, Mitch," she said. She thought of that tub of Coronas in the car and the bag of limes and how years ago she'd always let him set the tone of their encounters. It hit her that she needed to find something of herself she'd lost. Something that her recent affairs had lacked. Something she suspected she'd given away when she'd betrayed Mitch.

"What kind of deal?" he asked. The waitress brought his second beer and he took a swallow.

"One weekend of love slavery."

There was a sparkle in his eye that told her he liked her plan. It had been a long time since she'd had this kind of fun—this kind of sexual excitement in her life.

"Who gets to be the master?" he asked. His hand fell on the back of her neck and she prayed he wouldn't move it. She was still aroused from that one kiss. One damned kiss and her panties were damp and she was ready to lie down for him.

"Me," she said. She needed to be the master. She needed to control him and use him as her sex toy for a weekend. Then maybe she'd reclaim what she'd lost and be able to move on.

"I don't think so," he said, caressing the side of her neck.

Of course he didn't. Mitch had never been malleable. Why would he suddenly start now? "What do you propose?"

"That we let our prowess decide."

His caressing finger was distracting and she decided two could play at that game. She dropped her hand to his thigh, kneading the firm muscle under the taut fabric of his pants. "Meaning?"

"Whoever wins in court is the master. Whoever loses the slave."

A vibration started in the center of her body and spread outward. "Will that satisfy you?"

IT WOULD TAKE MORE than a weekend to satisfy him, but his plans for vengeance might be quenched, or at least assuaged. He wanted her to feel the way he had. He didn't care if that was right or fair. And a weekend with Sophia was a good start.

"Counselor, you've got a deal."

First thing tomorrow morning he was going to be all over Florida case records like a rash. He'd have to have Deke and a couple of assistants come out from L.A. to help. But he was going to put together an airtight case. Not just to save Spinder's ass but to win this side wager.

He needed to have Sophia under his control. He even knew the first thing he'd make her do. Take off that damned suit and put on the velvet ribbon.

She fished her valet claim check from her purse and left some bills on the table. "Good. Well, I guess I'll get going, then."

He grabbed her hand to keep her from standing. He wasn't ready to go up to his room and deal with Dev's troubles. That was all that awaited him tonight, worry for a friend that he didn't know how to rescue from himself.

He did have a strategy meeting with Marcus, Jason's publicist. But that wasn't until later. He wanted to spend more time with Sophia, which he didn't examine too closely. "What's the hurry?"

"I've got work to do." She watched him with those wide blue eyes of hers, guarding her words.

"You work too much."

"How do you know?"

"You've got circles under your eyes," he said, tracing the fine purple shadows. Her skin was porcelain smooth and softer than the down pillows on his bed. He hadn't taken the time to notice earlier.

"You sure know the way to a girl's heart."

Her heart. Damned if he was going after that again. He'd learned the hard way that Sophia's heart was kept under lock and key and only a masochist would even try to get at it. And as kinky as he liked his sex, he'd never liked physical pleasure and emotional pain together. "I'm not interested in your heart."

She blanched and looked down at her purse. "No, you aren't."

What a bastard he could be. "Don't try to make me feel bad about that. I wanted your heart once upon a time."

She sighed and tilted her head to the side. Her careful gaze moved over his face and he knew she wasn't seeing him but the younger man he'd been. "But I was afraid to give it to you."

"Was it fear that stopped you? Funny, I thought it was greed." As arousal was dying down in his veins, anger was rising. Why were they talking about the past? It might be what brought them together tonight, but beyond that he didn't want to delve into it.

"Greed? Is that what you've thought of me all these years?"

"Babe, I respect you too much to tell you what I really thought of you."

"I don't blame you. I never should have lied to you," she said.

She'd never been a woman to try to manipulate a man and he'd trusted that sweet innocent face and of course that sexy body that he knew as well as his own.

"Why did you?" he asked before he could think better of it.

She twisted the valet claim check in her hands. He watched her try to find the words to answer him.

"I was losing myself, Mitch."

Never in a million years would he comprehend what she'd just said. She'd been in the top five at Harvard Law. Her mentor was one of the most powerful women in the law community and had in the intervening years become a Supreme Court Judge. Sophia had been a woman on the cusp of becoming very capable and powerful in her own right. For her to say she had feared losing herself sounded like a cop-out to him.

"I don't understand."

"You can't. You've always known who you were. Even when life shakes you up, you land on your feet."

She was the second person to say as much in less than three hours. He didn't like the sound of it. Sure he had a plan and nothing was going to stop him from achieving his goals. That didn't mean that life was any easier for him than it was for others.

"You had some pretty strong supporters at Harvard. And I've stumbled plenty of times."

"You look like you made it back to your feet."

"Of course I did. And I didn't have to shove anyone out of my way to do it." He had to get out of here before he did something really foolish like let her see how badly that had affected him.

He stood, tossed some bills on the table. "See you around, babe."

He walked out of the bar without a backward glance. The lobby was opulent and crowded. Mitch blended in with the businessmen returning from a day of meetings heading toward the elevator.

"Mitch?"

He stopped, but didn't turn around. He was still angry. More than angry—he was pissed and he'd never been one of those people who could be polite when he was mad. He knew he'd say something he'd regret especially if he turned around.

"I'm sorry," she said. "Maybe we should call the bet off."

He pivoted and walked over to her. "Babe, there's no way in hell we're calling that wager off. You're going to be mine for a weekend and when I leave you're going to miss me for a long, long time.''

The elevator car arrived and he walked away from the woman who'd given him the greatest joy in life, and the sharpest pain.

4

SOPHIA'S FIRST INSTINCT was to run away but she knew better than to start giving ground. So she did the only thing she could think of and went on the offensive. Mitch Hollaran wasn't going to make her doubt herself or the course she'd put them both on. And if she knew one thing about the woman she'd become it was that the scared emotional woman deep inside wasn't going to start having any say in any decision now.

She pivoted on her heel, intent on reaching her car and tormenting her old lover on the phone. He knew what buttons to push to make her respond and she knew likewise. This time with Mitch she wasn't a girl discovering fire in a man's arms for the first time. This time she was a woman in full control of her life and her body. She wasn't taking the passive role with any man.

She bumped into a man and paused to apologize. But found herself face-to-face with one of her co-workers, Joseph O'Neill. O'Neill had recently joined the office, moving to Orlando from Miami where he'd had an impressive record of wins. They were lucky to have him on their staff. Sophia had hired him and liked the fact that Joseph, though a family man, worked as hard as any other attorney in the office.

"O'Neill, sorry about that."

Joseph wasn't particularly tall but he was well built and he had thick mane of midnight-black hair that he kept closely trimmed. He was of Hispanic descent on his mother's side and looked like a young Andy Garcia.

"No problem, Deltonio. I should know to get out of your way when I see you coming."

She wasn't sure what he meant by that. Had she become too ruthless at work? And could a district attorney ever be too ruthless? "Having drinks with friends?"

"Not tonight. I'm meeting with Mueller. Want to join us?"

Sophia knew she had work to do...on her cases and with Mitch. But saying no to meeting with their boss wasn't something she could do. Her career plans were the most important in her life. "Sure."

Sophia reentered the Bösendorfer Lounge and wondered if Joan and O'Neill had been there while she'd had her drink with Mitch. She'd been totally focused on him and wouldn't have noticed if the Governor of Florida had sat down next to her.

"Look who I ran into in the lobby," O'Neill said. "Good evening, Sophia."

Joan was seated at the very table she and Mitch had sat at earlier. Joan was sitting in the same spot that Sophia had been in. O'Neill pulled up a chair, leaving Sophia Mitch's former spot.

"Joan. I was meeting with one of the attorneys on the Spinder case."

She knew it was impossible but she could still smell Mitch's aftershave. She closed her eyes for a second and inhaled deeply. Shivers raced through her and when she opened them she found Joan staring at her. The feeling that everything was spinning out of control hovered on the edge of her conscious.

"Good. Did you get the names of the other attorneys who'll be on the case?"

Was it her imagination or did O'Neill have too many teeth? If he smiled at her again she was going to be tempted to toss something at him. Sophia suddenly realized what this little meeting was about. And it wasn't the Spinder case though that was part of it. Joan was trolling around for another D.A. to move into the deputy slot if Sophia lost her edge.

No. Dammit, she hadn't discussed anything related to the case. "Of course."

"Joseph, will you go get us a couple of drinks. I'll have a White Zin and Sophia, Pinot Grigio?"

Sophia nodded. Joseph didn't look too happy at

being sent for drinks, but Sophia recognized this meeting and this moment for what it was. Usually Sophia envied her boss, the poise that she had and the life that she'd carved for herself, but sitting in this lounge at ten o'clock at night she realized that Joan lived for the law.

Did she ever get lonely? Had she ever made a sexy wager with an ex-lover? Probably not. Mueller was a single-minded woman when it came to her career, and she was everything Sophia had ever wanted to be.

Did she still want that? Of course she did. Sophia made up her mind to focus on her career. She hadn't really stopped focusing on it, she reminded herself. She'd only let Mitch Hollaran distract her for a millisecond and look what had happened. She vowed it wouldn't happen again.

"I've asked Joseph to move some of his caseload and assist you with this one," Joan said.

Sophia straightened up and banished Mitch Hollaran from her senses. "That's not necessary, Joan. I can handle this."

"Are you sure?" Joan asked.

Sophia bit her lip. "Of course I am. I've already scheduled an interview with Holly McBride and her family."

"Hollaran is a big gun and you were making noises this afternoon about not wanting the case."

"Well, I don't need help. I've got the case locked up. The trial's not for two months."

Joan leaned back in the seat and studied her. Sophia struggled not to squirm under the scrutiny.

"Something's off about you, Sophia."

"Nothing is off. I'm just tired."

"A vacation will fix that," Joan said, after a few minutes of silence had passed.

"Yes, it will."

"Sophia, I've always seen a lot of myself in you."

"I'm flattered."

"Don't be. I've made some tough choices, and I regret some of them."

"I'm not sure what you're trying to say."

"Only make sure you'll be happy living for the job. It's kind of lonely here and not everyone would be happy with it."

"Joan, you know me, I live for work."

"Actually, Deltonio, I'm not sure you know yourself," Joan said.

Joseph returned with the drinks before Sophia could comment. The conversation settled around the panty-raider case she'd won this afternoon, but Sophia didn't feel like celebrating. She knew that the next two months were going to be hard. Harder than she'd thought they'd be because Joan was right. She didn't know herself anymore. And that was never a good place to be.

MITCH HAD SPENT the last few hours on the phone trying to help Dev out. The best he could do was get Dev assigned to a very strict detox program that came with a twenty-four-hour-a-day counselor when you were released. The judge had promised if Dev used again he'd be in jail for a long time. Dev had muttered his thanks, but Mitch knew something still wasn't right with his friend.

He'd had a meeting with Marcus, Spinder's manager, to discuss strategy. The plan he and Marcus had come up with was for Jason to appear untouched by the trial. Jason would play the media with his usual finesse. Marcus booked Spinder on several talk shows over the weekend, and an officer of the court would accompany Jason on his out-of-town gigs, ensuring he didn't skip bail.

Mitch had a list of people to interview, mostly cast and crew members who'd been at the bar that night with Jason. At least one of the other guys had been out with Holly before.

In fact, Mitch thought, as he reentered his own room and prepared to relax for the evening, everything was going well. Still, he was too wired to sleep. He paced over to the window. Glancing out at the Orlando skyline he saw his own reflection in the glass.

Mitch wished he really were the man he saw in the glass. The reflection looked successful. And if he could stop at success Mitch wouldn't have any problems.

But there was no escaping the demons pushing him forward, nor the knowledge that revenge wasn't the solution he was searching for and that even leaving Sophia in the same state he'd been in years ago wasn't going to turn his life around.

He cursed and turned on his heel. Maybe he'd go to the weight room and work off some of this tension that lingered from his meeting with Sophia.

He wished he hadn't let his anger get the better of him with Sophia. If he'd kept his mouth shut he probably would have been able to coax her up to his suite for the kind of reunion they'd both wanted.

But a few hours in the sack weren't going to give him the kind of satisfaction he wanted. He needed to take Sophia's well-ordered world and make it into chaos. He cursed again and decided against working out. He went to the minibar and pulled out a Heineken. Twisting off the cap, he took a long draw from the bottle.

He turned off the lights and moved his chair in front of the window. Propping his feet on the sill, he watched the lights for a while and tried to ignore the images in his head. Tried to tune out Stevie Ray Vaughan's electric guitar riffs and the woman who was swaying to the music wearing nothing but a sexy smile.

But the image wouldn't leave and he leaned back and let Sophia seduce him here in the privacy of his room where only he would know about it. His cock twitched, tension spread throughout his body and he knew he should have left the room earlier, rather than staying here with the memories.

But this was part of his nightly routine ever since learning he'd be coming to Orlando and facing the woman who'd changed him. He'd been living with memories of everything he'd done with her. He'd been mostly focusing on the sex and the ending because if he remembered how good it had been between them he might start wanting something else. Something he knew better than to want because it wasn't real.

The only real things were cases fought in a court of law, and old friendships. And he and Sophia weren't old friends. They were ex-lovers with bad blood between them.

Remember that, old man, he reminded himself. Tilting back the bottle he drained it. He thought about having another one but wasn't planning on getting drunk tonight when he had so much work to do tomorrow. So he focused on planning his next move on Sophia.

His next gift was sure to rattle her. It was from day two of their long-ago winter break vacation. Four days of nonstop sex and blues music. Back then, Mitch had planned the four days to lead up to a marriage proposal. But on the fifth day he'd found himself on a wild goose chase and at the end of his relationship with Sophia. He still had that damned engagement ring.

Day two had been a picnic inside their apartment. His gift contained everything they'd used that second day. A small wicker picnic-style basket with Polaroid instant camera, a cashmere throw, a bottle of tequila, margarita mix, two margarita glasses, a box of salt, flavored tortilla chips, salsa and a Jimmy Buffett CD.

This time he planned to be in her office when the basket arrived. He'd order it to be delivered during the meeting he had scheduled with her tomorrow afternoon. This revenge thing was more fun than he'd anticipated. And more provocative.

The phone rang, startling him. He glanced at the clock. It was ten minutes to midnight. Only a little before nine West Coast time.

"Hollaran."

He heard nothing but the sounds of deep breathing and a radio being played. Suddenly the song on the radio came in more clearly. Stevie Ray Vaughan singing ''Things That I Used To Do.'' His gut clenched because one of the things he and Sophia used to do every day when they got home was have oral sex.

He could feel the brush of her hair over his stomach and thighs. His cock hardened even more. He reached for the zipper on his jeans and carefully lowered it to give his growing erection more room.

He waited, listening to the song, knowing Sophia was on the other end of the line.

''Still there?'' she asked, her voice low and husky.

As if he'd have hung up on her. Maybe he should have but they were playing a game of one-upmanship and he'd thought he had the upper hand. Sophia had just proven she was in the game.

''I'm here, babe.''

''Just wanted to make sure you were thinking of me tonight.''

''I am. Damn, that song brings back so many memories. Are you listening to the CD I sent?''

''Yes. What have you been doing since I left?''

''Working and remembering.''

''Remembering what?''

''The way you looked naked.''

''Good.''

''Yeah, you are good when you're naked.''

"I've never thought about it that way. I thought I was wicked."

"You have your moments," he said, as the wail of the bass echoed over the line and he shivered wishing he was with Sophia.

"Remember the time we drove all night to get to the beach and see the sunrise?"

"I remember every time," he said with more honesty than he'd planned to reveal to her. They'd made love in the dunes with the waves crashing behind them. It had been the moment he'd known for sure that he wanted to keep Sophia in his life forever.

"Me too," she said and abruptly the sounds of Vaughan's music shut off. He heard a wind chime and the sounds of Sophia's footsteps.

"Sophia?"

She said nothing. What she was doing? What she was wearing? Why had she called?

Maybe she wanted some revenge against him. He hoped she'd come to the same conclusion he had. Revenge was a double-edged sword, and there was no such thing as distance when it came to the sexual kind.

SOPHIA HUNG ON THE LINE, not sure what to say to Mitch. God, she needed to forget about the softer side of their relationship, but for some reason Mitch was dredging that all up. But she wasn't backing down now. Why had she brought up the memory of the beach?

Making love in the dunes had been magical and when he'd cradled her close against his strong chest afterward, she'd realized she was losing herself, and that she'd gladly stay lost if it meant she could always lie in his arms.

That basket he'd sent her sat on the kitchen counter. Despite the fact that she'd turned off the CD, she could still hear that sexy low beat in her head. Sex-music. That's what she'd always thought of it as. It beat through her body with each breath she took and she felt as though she was vibrating in time with it.

And she wanted to have sex now. She didn't want to use her vibrator to bring release, she wanted sweaty body sex with Mitch.

Dammit. She'd had a vague plan to tease Mitch the way he had with that basket he'd sent. They had the same memories so she'd thought the song and a few teasing words over the phone would be an effective volley in the game they were playing.

But her plan had backfired.

It didn't matter that he'd sounded vulnerable just then on the phone. Emotions had no place in her life now. She was a single woman who enjoyed the life she'd created for herself and no man was going to push her off track. Especially not Mitch.

"Sophia?" he asked again.

She busied herself in the kitchen. Checking the teapot and finding it full. She turned on the burner. "Sorry. You threw me off track with your honesty."

"Why? I've always been honest with you."

He had. And that had plagued her for longer than he'd believe if she told him about it. Mitch carried his truth and honor like a banner and it had made her question her own integrity many times. "But we're adversaries now."

He sighed. What was he wearing? "Babe, I think we always have been."

"I didn't realize that."

"That's because you look at the world through Sophia-tinted glasses."

She didn't like the sound of that. She was a realist and always had been. True, when she'd first arrived at Harvard she'd been a little bit sheltered, but it hadn't taken her long to lose that naïveté. "What's that mean?"

"That you see what you want to and ignore the rest."

"What didn't I see?"

"That love isn't always a happy thing."

"Did you really know that?"

"Not until I left Cambridge."

His words were a blow. And she knew they shouldn't have been because she'd made her peace with her past and had moved on. Or had she? Because if she'd moved on she shouldn't be feeling this...hell, what was she feeling? Damn, Mitch Hollaran and Jason Spinder. Her life was so uncomplicated before this case had landed on her desk.

"I didn't call to rehash the past."

"I know why you called," he said.

"You do?" She shouldn't have been surprised. There was a connection between herself and Mitch that no amount of distance or time could diminish.

"I do," he said, his voice deepening. "Having trouble getting to sleep tonight?"

"No. I always work late."

"But you weren't working tonight, were you?" he asked, again in that deep voice of his that stroked over her aroused senses and made blood pool deep in her body.

How had the tables turned? She'd hoped to be the one disturbing him with erotic images. "I was working tonight."

That was the truth. She'd been working until her neck had gotten stiff from sitting too long. And then she'd spotted the Coronas and the Stevie Ray CD on the kitchen counter. She'd been unable to resist putting the CD on and opening a bottle of Corona.

From there, everything had spiraled out of her control.

"Methinks the lady doth protest too much."

"Don't quote Shakespeare, you don't like him."

"But you like him, babe. And you like to hear him late at night...after."

Hang up. Now.

This wasn't going the way she planned and he was making her remember things she'd rather forget. Sex was okay because her rational mind understood needs and wants. But she didn't want to remember Mitch's deep voice reading her sonnets in the middle of the night. That had nothing to do with sex.

"But it's not after," she said, her voice betraying more than she would have liked.

"Isn't that why you called, Sophia? A little phone sex to up the ante in this game we're playing."

"Yes."

"Then let's get to it. I was sitting in the dark thinking of you when you called."

"God, Mitch. Don't be vulnerable to me."

"I thought we covered that, babe. I know you're a barracuda and I don't intend to get bitten again."

She bit her lower lip. *Phone sex.* It had seemed so simple but now she didn't know where to begin. Or even if she should. In the past, she'd have let Mitch do it all.

Even when she'd been the aggressor in their love-making he'd been the one to urge her to be. She'd never started anything with him before. Or for that matter with any of the other men she'd had affairs with.

"Are you naked?" she asked, after a few minutes. This wasn't about Mitch. This was about her. And not being vulnerable to the past anymore.

"Just about. I'm wearing a pair of jeans. You?"

"Just a T-shirt," she said. A faded cotton one of Mitch's that she should've thrown out a long time ago, but had never been able to part with.

"What are you wearing underneath it?" he asked in a raspy voice that told her it wouldn't take long for him to go over.

"Nothing."

"Babe, you're killing me."

"Good," she said laughing for the first time since that basket had landed on her desk. "Now here's what I want you to do. Take off your jeans and climb on the bed."

"Only if you do the same."

She switched off the teapot and walked down the hall to her bedroom. She turned on the lamp on the nightstand and stripped off her T-shirt. She could see her own body in the mirrored closet doors. Her nipples were already peaked and her body was slightly flushed.

"Can you see yourself, Mitch?"

"In the mirror over the dresser I can."

"Describe what you see," she ordered.

His voice was deep and luscious as he described his own body.

"I'm rubbing my hand over my chest, the way you used to do. Remember my scar?"

In her mind she knew exactly where that scar was. Right above his left nipple. She'd spent hours caressing it. He'd gotten the mark when he tried to ride his bike off the picnic table in back of his house when he'd been ten.

Mitch's body was actually covered in small scars from numerous daring adventures. She'd never tried anything that held the threat of danger. She liked her life neat and orderly.

"Babe?"

"I'm still here. I'd like to lick that spot. I know how it turns you on. Is your nipple tightening?"

"Yes."

"Good, now pinch it lightly."

"Just like I do to you?"

"Oh, yes. Just like that," she said.

"You do the same," he said. She did. Sliding her hands over the full curves of her breasts and pinching her nipples lightly. His breathing increased.

She imagined her hands moving over his lightly hairy chest. She knew the way the hair there tickled against her fingers. She moved over him in her mind. Let her full breasts brush against his warm chest. Felt the hardness between her legs. In her mind he was starting to sweat.

Her breathing grew deeper. "Sophia?"

"I'm there with you. I'm straddling your hips. God, you're hot and hard."

"Harder than I've ever been before. And you're wet, Sophia. Very wet."

"I am," she agreed.

"I'm going to take you now, Mitch. Take you deep inside me. You fill me so completely."

"I do. I feel like I belong there. Inside you."

"You do," she agreed. She clenched her vagina, sliding her hand down between her legs and masturbating to the image in her head and the sounds of her lover on the other end of the phone. She heard his breath rasping out of his teeth and then a deep groan that she knew signaled his release. Her own breathing grew heavier and she thrust two fingers deep into her sheath until she climaxed.

She lay back on the pillows and heard Mitch breathing on the other end of the phone. She felt closer to him than she had to any person in a long time. She wished she'd stayed at his hotel. Wished she'd followed him on the elevator and wished she was lying next to him right now. Wished she could feel his warmth surrounding her and reminding her she was no longer alone.

"Night, babe," Mitch said and disconnected the

phone. A wave of coldness covered her and her reflection in the mirrored doors reminded her she was still all alone. Not wanting to face her reflection any longer, Sophia cradled the cordless unit next to her breasts and rolled over on her side.

5

SOPHIA DELTONIO, *Assistant District Attorney*, the brass plate read and Mitch hesitated outside the door. Hanging up the phone last night had been the hardest thing he'd done in a long time. He'd wanted to stay on the line and talk to her. Maybe quote one of those damned Shakespeare sonnets he'd memorized half a lifetime ago, but had never been able to forget.

But he wasn't building a relationship with his future wife. He'd been indulging in a sensual game of war. Since vengeance and revenge weren't games that civilized men played with nice women, he'd felt more than his share of guilt this morning. He knew he was the winner in last night's skirmish, but he didn't feel flushed with victory.

He tried to recall all the reasons why he'd settled on this course of action, but this afternoon standing in the bustling hallway of the Orange County District Attorney's office, they weren't easy to recall. As he stood here in the heat of the Orlando summer his reasons for revenge came back to him. This wasn't where he'd thought they'd end up. He knew no matter how many women he slept with or how many cases he won in court, he wasn't going to be satisfied until he'd won against Sophia.

The FedEx guy came down the hall, paused in front of Sophia's office and entered. He'd timed his arrival just right. And the plans he'd made earlier that had seemed so sleek were now making him feel a little sleazy. He took some comfort from the fact that Sophia had made a sexual wager with him. She was as eager as he was to find some resolution to the past.

And she had called him last night, he reminded himself. Perhaps she was only looking for sex. No perhaps about it. He knew her work was the most important thing in her life and Sophia had proven that no man—especially Mitch Hollaran—was going to come between her and her career.

He strolled through the opened doorway with a nonchalance he was far from feeling. A pretty young brunette glanced up at him. She smiled in welcome. Her nameplate said Alice Smith.

She finished signing for the FedEx package before turning to him. She was dressed in a thin rayon dress that ended well above her knees and showed her curvy little body perfectly. She caught him staring at her legs and winked at him.

Here was an uncomplicated woman. But Mitch

wasn't interested. He was only looking because, hey, he was a guy and pretty legs were pretty legs.

"Can I help you?" she asked.

"Hello, Alice. I'm Mitch Hollaran. I have a two-thirty appointment with Sophia."

"Have a seat, Mr. Hollaran, and I'll let her know you're here. Would you like something to drink?"

"No thanks."

The FedEx delivery guy exited the office. Alice carried the large brown box into Sophia's office and, he assumed, announced him. The package could be anything, but Mitch knew what it contained. Knew the memories it would evoke and was counting on them to rattle the sleek sophisticated woman he was about to face in the courtroom.

Last night though he'd been reminded that there was a softer woman underneath. He slipped his hand into his pocket and caressed that thin velvet ribbon. One piece of ribbon was his only reminder that Sophia wasn't the woman she presented to the world.

"She'll see you now," Alice said.

Mitch shifted his briefcase to his left hand and entered Sophia's office. The late-afternoon sun streamed into her office. The walls were crammed with bookshelves piled up with books. He skimmed the walls searching for the Monet print he remembered from their time together, but when he didn't see it he felt a little better about his behavior last night and about having the picnic basket delivered to her today.

"Hello, Sophia." She looked too good to him, though she wore the trappings of a corporate amazon—a dark blue power suit, and her thick curly hair was tightly pulled back at the base of her neck. But her eyes looked weary.

"Good afternoon, Mitch. This just arrived from you."

"Going to open it?" he asked. He steeled himself against the wave of sympathy rolling over him. This was the woman who'd called him for phone sex. This was the woman who was counting on using her feminine wiles to win the private battle they were waging.

She hesitated as she placed her hands over the package. That Corona basket must have startled her more than he thought if she was afraid to open this box.

"Scared?" he taunted. Damn, he felt savage today. He had an evening flight to L.A. It was a good thing he was leaving Orlando for a few days because otherwise he might do something rash. Something he'd regret.

"Of you?" she asked in that clipped tone he'd come to know so well yesterday afternoon in the courtroom.

He shrugged. It made no difference what she said, he knew trepidation when he saw it. He'd made a career of reading clients, jurors and judges. Her body language said she was trying to put up barriers to protect herself.

He put his briefcase on the guest chair and walked around her desk. She was seated in a high-back executive leather chair. He leaned one hip against the surface of her cherrywood desk. Right next to the box.

"I don't think so."

"I know so, Sophia. I think you're scared to look in the box because you know I'm right."

"The only thing I know is that you are too cocky for your own good," she said. Taking her paper cutter from the blotter, she stood and carefully cut the tape seam on the box.

"Wonder what it is?" he asked.

"No. I'm only opening it now because I want you to see that nothing you do can rattle me."

He crossed his arms over his chest and waited. She opened the box and pushed the filler paper out of the way. Mitch didn't take his gaze from her face and when she pulled out the picnic basket her face froze. Her hands shook as she opened the wicker flap and looked inside.

The victory was hollow for him when she sank to her chair and closed her eyes. Winning at this game with a coldhearted manipulator was one thing. Hurting the only woman he'd ever let himself care about was something else.

THE MEMORIES ASSOCIATED with this basket were too strong. They reminded her of the family she'd fought to escape from and the man who'd made it so easy for her to depend on him. This basket was a perfect reminder of why she'd sent Mitch on that false trail that had ultimately led to the ending of their relationship.

The basket also represented all that had been right with them. She didn't want to explore that, especially with Mitch standing so close she could feel his body heat and smell the spicy-musk scent of his aftershave, the same one he had used in college. Damn the man.

He wore his hand-made suit with the ease that some men wore khakis and buttondown shirts. His dark hair was neatly combed and his steely gray eyes made her feel defenseless as he watched her. She hardened herself against that gaze that made her feel as if he could see right through her, but a part of her—the part that she'd left behind in Cambridge all those years ago—reveled in the attention and craved more of it.

She realized suddenly what he was doing. The picnic had taken place on the second day of their winter break holiday. She had a bad feeling in the pit of her stomach.

He knew what he was doing to her and she had the feeling she'd just lost some ground, but she didn't regret it. She'd come to play, and sometimes in order to win the game you had to lose the match.

"Sophia?" he asked. He sounded concerned and she glanced up at him.

She thought she saw some compassion in his eyes and knew she saw the first tinge of arousal there. Good, he remembered too. She wasn't surprised. Last night she'd learned a powerful lesson, one that she'd learned in high school science but she'd never thought to apply to interpersonal relationships until now—until Mitch.

Every action has an equal reaction. And the reaction between the two of them had always been off the Richter scale. How could she have forgotten that?

Had she been insane when she'd suggested their wager? No. She wanted him as her love slave. She wanted to be the one in control of him and his luscious body so she could get him out of her system. She wanted to never again feel the intense vulnerability she felt at this moment as she stared into the past and felt his eyes on her.

She tried to find the words to sound flip, but she couldn't. She remembered the picnic they'd gone on with that old cashmere blanket that had been her grandmother's. The wicker picnic basket had been old and faded, the latch broken, and they'd filled it with the same Key West items he had in there. They'd pushed all the furniture to the one side of their apartment and taped up pictures of the Keys from travel brochures. Then, using their old blender they'd made a huge pitcher of margaritas and made love on the cashmere blanket with Jimmy Buffett playing in the background.

"Still like margaritas?" he asked.

"Yes," she said, softly.

Though she hadn't had one since she'd sipped the salty drink from his lips all those years ago. Her mouth watered remembering the taste and the sensation. Before Mitch she'd never imagined anything as mundane as margaritas and salt as tools to seduction, but he'd turned everything into them.

He reached and touched her face. He slid one long tapered finger down the side of her cheek and neck, resting on the pulse beating strongly at the base of her neck. He then circled his finger against her skin. Shivers of awareness spread down her body. Her nipples tightened against her smooth satin bra and her panties dampened at the crotch.

One touch was all it took. Of course it didn't help matters that last night had primed her for this. For him.

"I miss that ribbon you used to wear," he said, his finger tracing the line that the velvet used to form on her neck.

"It wasn't very professional."

She rested her hand on his thigh and felt the muscles contract under her hand. She kneaded his leg through the cloth of his pants, tracing random patterns that brought her closer and closer to his groin until she saw his erection strain against his zipper.

"No, it wasn't. And you're all about professionalism these days, right?"

He slid his finger down the V of her blouse. His touch was light but the heat burned through her skin. He deftly unfastened the top button and slipped his finger under the silk fabric. He rubbed her right nipple with one finger. Light touches that circled and circled, bringing her closer to the edge.

"Hmm-mmm."

He undid the rest of her buttons and pushed the fabric of her blouse aside. The bra she wore today was a lightly patterned creamy color with demi-cups.

"Very nice."

She smiled at him. Mitch had always liked lingerie. She'd never tell him but she'd worn this matching bra and panty set today because he'd been on her mind as she dressed. Usually at work she was no-nonsense from her skin out. But not today.

"I scheduled this meeting to let you know I'm going back to L.A. for a few days. Then I'll be setting up a temporary office here. I'll forward that information to you as soon as I have it."

"Okay. Why are you telling me this?"

"I want to get the business out of the way."

Taking the blanket from the basket, he stood and walked around the desk. "What are you doing?"

"Giving us some privacy," he said. He walked to the office door and locked the handle, then turned back to her. He pushed the guest chairs to the side and spread the blanket on the floor. From his knees he held his hand out to her and gave her a wicked grin. "Indulge me?"

She bit her lower lip and knew only one thing. She wasn't going to be a victim to her desires or to Mitch Hollaran. She stood and walked over to him.

MITCH HAD MEANT for the basket to be another reminder of her betrayal of him, of how unexpected her behavior had been. The sensual game he'd planned before leaving L.A., but something had changed since his reunion with Sophia. He needed her. And he knew from the way she'd reacted last night to his voice and this afternoon to his touch that she needed him too.

As she approached him he pushed aside thoughts of keeping score and how even things should be. He focused solely on the only woman who could seduce him with a look. Her breasts strained the cups of the demi-bra she wore.

"Got that CD I sent you?" he asked.

"It's in my car. I didn't bring it in because..."

"Because..."

"I didn't want to think about you at work," she said after a brief pause.

"Did it work?" he asked. He'd been trying to keep her from his mind all day, and despite long meetings with Jason Spinder and Marcus he hadn't been successful. The sounds she'd made last night as she'd climaxed echoed in his mind and he wanted to hear them again.

"Until you showed up with that damned sexy smile of yours and your gift from the past."

"Want to throw me out?"

"What do you think?"

He leaned back on his elbows to stare at her. Starting at her trim ankles perched on the top of very conservative pumps, he skimmed his gaze to the hem of her skirt that ended a respectable inch above her knee. Despite the primness of her clothing, she set him on fire. Maybe it was the sleek curves underneath or the spark of mischief in her eyes, but he knew that he'd never look at her in a business suit again and not picture her just as she stood before him.

"I think this isn't too bad. Though I was hoping for a little striptease to 'Shake For Me.'"

"That's not in the cards for you unless you win in court and I become your love slave."

"I intend for you to be mine," he said. The words revealed more than he'd intended. He did want her to be completely his when he left her. And this time since he was going to be the one leaving, she was going to feel the same desolation he'd felt.

His instincts were running the show now and any plans he'd made or any chance he had of keeping some sort of distance from her vanished. She stood in front of him in a way he'd imagined her a million times since the night they'd parted. He couldn't wait to taste her skin again. To feel the hard buds of her aroused nipples under his tongue. To sink his fingers into the humid warmth of her center and make her come for him.

"Be yours?"

"For one weekend."

"Is one weekend really going to be enough?" she asked.

Hell, he didn't know. And frankly at this moment he didn't care. He wanted nothing more than to sate himself with her, to put to rest past hurts and melt into her until he forgot everything but the way she felt against him.

"Do you want to lengthen the internment?" he

countered. He doubted one weekend was going to be long enough to work her out of his system. He had this image in his head of her tied to his bed. Waiting for him when he came home from work.

''Why are you smiling like that?''

''Just imagining you as my slave,'' he said.

''Don't make too many plans, Mitch. I'm very confident that you'll be mine.''

He stood up and walked to the woman who'd held sway over him for too many years. He spanned her waist with his hands and lifted her to the desk. To hell with this rekindling of old fires. There was a new blaze running through his body that said to hell with the past.

''What's this?'' she asked. She slowly unbuttoned his shirt. He'd forgotten what her touch on his chest felt like. Her fingers were long and she touched him as if she were rediscovering something precious that had been lost.

She leaned down and brushed her lips against his pecs and a fine tremble started at the base of his spine, rolling through his body. His cock was so engorged that he had to close his eyes and take a deep breath to keep from coming in his pants.

''Counselor?'' she asked, her voice soft and seductive. She bit him lightly, then soothed the small pain with her tongue.

Incapable of speech, he grunted at her. His mind had shut down the moment he'd touched her.

"I asked what this was," she said against his skin. He caged her head in his hands and rubbed his chest against her mouth.

"This is aggressive negotiation."

She blew on his nipple, then daintily licked him. "Who's the aggressor?"

He looked down on the tops of her tanned breasts, pushing urgently against the cups of her bra. Each breath she took threatened to force them to spill out of the cups yet they didn't. "I am."

He skimmed his hands down under her skirt, pushing the garment to her waist. She wore thigh-high hose and her panties matched her bra.

He reached between her legs and touched her lightly through the silk of her underwear. The gusset was damp and he could smell her arousal. Leaning down he pushed his face against her and inhaled deeply.

She pushed her fingers into his hair and held him against her, her hips moving toward him. He pushed the crotch of her panties to the side and parted her nether lips carefully, exposing her clitoris. It was full and red.

He exhaled deeply, letting his breath caress her first, and then sampled her with his tongue. Her taste was a remembered delicacy. Sweet and salty and uniquely Sophia. He teased her with the tip of his tongue and heard her moan deep in her throat.

"Hold yourself open for me, babe," he said.

Her hands left his head and she slid them down her own body, holding herself open for his tender ministrations. He shoved two fingers deep into her body and let his other hand roam up over her breasts. Plucking at her nipples, he brought her closer to the edge of insanity with his mouth and other hand.

God, he'd missed this. Missed the way she responded to him as if he was the most man she'd ever had love her. Like he was the only man she wanted to love her. Like he was the only man meant to love her.

He forced those thoughts from his mind and concentrated instead on the sounds she was making in the back of her throat. He felt the minute contractions of her body around his fingers, then her hands were in his hair again, pulling him closer as her thighs clenched around his head and her climax rocked through her.

He pulled his fingers from her body and stood, pulling her into his arms. Her legs wrapped around his hips and he could feel her heat through the layers of his pants and briefs. He was so hard he thought he might come just from the slight rocking of her body against his. His fingers were still damp with her moisture. She rubbed her hands up and down his back and it would be so easy to free himself and slip into her but he didn't.

Despite the way things seemed and the way he felt right now, Sophia Deltonio wasn't a woman he should ever let have the upper hand. This was revenge, he tried to remind himself. But he was having a hard time believing it any more.

6

SOPHIA BURIED HER HEAD in Mitch's chest and sought the cloak of self-control she'd always used to protect herself. She'd had good sex before so it made no sense that this time in her office with Mitch should leave her feeling so...dammit, vulnerable.

She was determined not to let him see it. She closed her eyes one last time, breathing in his scent and brushing her lips against his chest. Hmm, he tasted good. Salty and warm.

Even knowing she was at work, she couldn't work up any real regret. This had been missing from her life for too long. Though she wasn't going to ever let Mitch know his reappearance had made her feel alive again.

She leaned back and tried for the kind of smile that would make him believe this was something that happened every day.

"Nice," she said. Damn, her voice sounded breathless.

"Yeah, nice," he said.

His erection still nudged against her. She wasn't

sure where the greater power lay. Should she return the favor and bring him to a climax or leave him wanting?

There was no decision to make. She wanted him. And she wasn't going to be the only one who had been left bare and vulnerable by her own orgasm. She unfastened her skirt and pushed it down her legs with her damp and torn panties.

Mitch raised one eyebrow but said nothing. She wedged her hands inside the waistband of his pants and briefs and pushed them down. He made her feel very womanly and feminine. Something that no other man had done. She'd always been the tough-as-nails prosecutor to them. But to Mitch she was always a woman first.

He held her hips easily in his large hands and stared down at her. The heat of his touch burned through her. She rocked against his erection.

"Not yet," he said through clenched teeth.

He rubbed her back in soothing circles, but she was still aroused from earlier. Still sensitized from his touch, she wasn't completely satisfied, and wouldn't be until he was hilt-deep inside her body. But she wasn't ready for more than one breach today. She needed to keep things even between her and Mitch. For sanity's sake she didn't want to return to old patterns of behavior that would leave her aching, and in the end, alone.

She reached between them and took his cock in her hand. He moaned as her fingers surrounded him. He was fully engorged and very hot to the touch. She caressed him with her entire hand, reaching down to tease his balls with the tips of her fingers. He lowered his head and took one of her nipples into his mouth, suckling strongly.

She leaned down and nibbled his shoulder with her teeth. His hands smoothed down her stomach, stopping at her belly button to tease and tickle her.

She felt her control waning. She knew if she didn't stop him, Mitch would take the lead again, leaving her helpless to the desire he called so easily from her.

"Not yet, Mitch. I want you to watch."

He sighed against her skin. Nipping playfully at her nipple, he sent an electric wave through her that ended at her clit. He straightened and stared at her hands on his body.

She continued to stroke her fingers over him. A small drop leaked from the slit at the top. She smoothed it under her fingers and down his length. She alternated her strokes from tugging him so hard he leaned up on his toes to softly tickling his length with the softest brush of only her fingertips.

His breathing was coming faster and she knew he was close to the edge. "Don't come yet."

Using the tips of her fingernails, she carefully

pricked his sac. He tightened and she knew he was close to the edge. He was going to blow at any moment.

She continued to tease him with her hand, bringing him nearer to the climax he sought. She lay back on the desk, taking her hands from his body. She smoothed them up over her stomach, lingering as he had at her belly button then up to the mounds of her breasts. She cupped them and smiled at Mitch who watched her with narrowed eyes.

"Come on me."

He groaned and spurted across her belly all the way to her ribs and the bottom of her breasts. He gripped her thighs in his strong fingers and thrust up over her until the last shudders of his climax rocked him. He leaned forward, his lean belly brushing hers. He covered her completely.

She reached for the box of tissues she kept on the edge of the desk to wipe herself clean but he stopped her. "Do something for me?"

"What?" she asked. But deep inside her heart had started beating harder and she knew what he was going to say. Something they'd done only twice before. Something that had made her feel like she was his. Like he'd marked her. God, was he marking her again?

Was it too late to protect herself from him? She had the sinking feeling it might be, and knew that no matter what she'd told herself she wasn't over this California man. Deep inside her a new fear arose. Maybe she never would be over him.

"Wear me?"

She bit her lip and nodded, unable to say the words that would reveal just how vulnerable she was to him. He rubbed his semen into her skin. He rubbed his hands over her breasts and ribs. The fluid dried quickly, tightening her skin.

He helped her from her desk. He dressed her in the quiet of the office, buttoning her blouse and fastening her skirt. He turned his back to her and dressed quickly. In a matter of minutes he was picking up his briefcase.

It was hard to believe her office wasn't a shambles but her desk showed no evidence that they'd just made love on it except for the FedEx box lying on the floor. The basket was still open on her chair.

Mitch tipped her chin back and dropped the sweetest kiss on her lips.

"See you around," he said and turned to leave.

THE FREEWAY WASN'T too crowded on Sunday morning as Mitch drove to his parents' house in Malibu. It had been two extremely long days since he'd left Sophia in her office. He'd seen the reflexive way she'd wrapped her arms around her waist and he knew that he'd wounded her by his callous comment as he'd left.

Mitch regretted his behavior, but old anger had toughened him where Sophia was concerned, or so he thought. When he'd returned home, her presence had continued to haunt him in his bedroom. This time, not the image of the college girl who'd broken his heart, but a woman with soulful eyes.

Being in his empty mansion in Bel Air had reaffirmed why he'd wanted to get Sophia out of his system. The place was too big for one man. He wanted a family but hadn't been able to trust any woman since Sophia. In fact, he'd kept a penthouse apartment for his affairs instead of allowing them to live in his home. He wasn't sure his present course of action was helping much.

He was obsessed with her again. Two of his old girlfriends had called him last night and invited him to go clubbing. He'd gone, but after an hour knew it was no use. He wasn't really the kind of man who liked to play the field. He knew himself well enough to know that he wasn't going to be satisfied with any other woman except Sophia.

He could only hope it was a temporary aberration because he was getting too old to stay single. He'd craved a family for a long time. Being a doting uncle to his nephews was fine, but he wanted his own kids.

He wanted to teach them to surf in the Pacific where his dad had taught him and Mark.

But before he could start a family of his own he had to put his demons from the past to rest. He'd been planning his next gift to her. He wasn't going to be swayed from his course of action. Revenge wasn't a quest he'd taken up lightly.

He pulled into his parents' subdivision and his cell phone chirped at him. He glanced down, seeing that he had a new voice-mail message.

He retrieved the message and heard…Stevie Ray Vaughan playing. Just the blues guitar licks and hard-pounding drums. Then Vaughan's voice singing ''Couldn't Stand the Weather.'' Mitch pulled to the side of the road and leaned back in his seat, listening to the song until it was over. There was no message, just the click of the telephone.

He dialed her number. She answered on the third ring.

''Hello?'' Her voice was soft and feminine. Not at all the businesslike tone she used in her office. He knew then that he was wrong to think that revenge was the only solution for them. Sophia was still that girl who wore poet shirts and a velvet ribbon around her neck.

He almost hung up. This wasn't the image of Sophia he wanted to foster. He liked her as the tough-as-nails prosecutor. A barracuda that sent men scurrying from her path.

"Is anyone there?" she asked. There was no music playing in the background this time.

"It's Mitch." He could hear her footsteps and he wondered what her house looked like.

"Are you calling about the case?" she asked.

"I'm returning your call."

She clucked her tongue at him and in his mind he could see her smile. Sophia was in a playful mood. "How do you know I called you?"

"Are you saying you didn't?" he asked.

"I'm taking the fifth, counselor," she said. He knew her eyes were sparkling and he wished he were in Orlando so he could go to her place and turn that mischief into desire. Mutual orgasms were fine, but he wanted to bury himself deep inside there and stay there until he had calmed the restless part of his soul that clamored for Sophia.

"The fifth...I've got a fifth of whiskey if you confess."

"Tsk tsk, bribing a witness. I'm not sure I like your ethics."

"I could care less about you liking my ethics."

She sighed. And it hurt him to hear the sound. Why it should matter to him that he'd caused her stress, he didn't know. Revenge, he reminded himself. But revenge was a double-edged sword and he felt as though he was bleeding from self-inflicted wounds. "I know."

"Listen, Sophia—"

"I'm trying to play by your rules," she said, interrupting him.

He knew he shouldn't let her change the subject. But he did. She's a big girl, he reminded himself. But just then she hadn't sounded like the tough assistant D.A. he'd seen on CNN last night. She'd sounded like the girl who used to wear that damned velvet ribbon. "I wasn't aware that I had rules."

"Yes, you are aware. I know what you're doing."

"What am I doing?" he asked because even he wasn't sure anymore.

"Seducing me."

"You can only be seduced if you want to be, Sophia."

"I don't think that's true," she said, her playfulness totally gone.

"Would seduction be so bad?" he asked after a few moments had passed.

"Not if you were just after sex."

"What makes you think I'm not?"

"The gift baskets. They're all from winter break right before…"

Right before she'd betrayed him. She didn't say it and he wasn't going to. He didn't like being reminded that he'd been so easily duped. "Most women would be flattered a guy remembered stuff like that.''

''I'm not most women.''

''No, you're not. You never have been.''

''What am I to you?''

He didn't know. She was an object he'd fixated on and he knew himself well enough to know that he wasn't going to be satisfied with less than total surrender.

''I can't keep doing this. I'm not going to play this game with you. We made a wager. Let's play this out in court and then let the winner take control.'' Sophia's voice was flat.

''Sophia, I'm not sure I can let it go,'' he said.

''Why not? It's because of the past. You want your pound of flesh, don't you?''

''Yes.''

''You've gotten it.''

''When?'' he asked.

''Friday when you left me with that 'see you around' comment.''

He cursed under his breath. ''I can be a bastard sometimes.''

''I'm no angel.''

He was swamped with the image of her spread out on her desk staring up at him. ''Thank God.''

She sighed again. ''I wish we didn't have the past between us.''

"Me too," he said, realizing it was true. This new Sophia—she brought to the fore dreams that he'd thought he'd left behind.

He knew then that he was right. The girl with the velvet ribbon was still a big part of the woman she'd become. As he pulled to a stop in front of his parents' house he knew that he didn't want revenge on that girl anymore.

SOPHIA HAD an early-morning meeting with Joan on Monday to talk about the Spinder case. She'd spent the rest of the weekend coming to peace with the fact that Mitch was back in her life.

She met her boss at a restaurant near Joan's house in Metro West. Le Crepe was a breakfast-only joint. Sophia was running late and had to speed to make it on time. She felt an incredible rush of adrenaline as she neared the exit, glanced down at the clock, and saw she'd made it on time. After she'd gotten off the phone with Mitch, she'd had a hard time sleeping last night.

From her career she'd learned it was a bad move to let someone else see weaknesses, and Mitch was the last guy she wanted to know she had any chinks in her armor. She sensed he knew though, whether she revealed them or not.

She cranked up AC/DC as she neared the strip-mall where the restaurant was. She needed to be at the top of her game today. Roaring lyrics and screaming guitars made her blood pump heavier and she closed her eyes for a second, visualizing herself winning the Spinder case in court.

She pulled the rearview mirror over and checked her lipstick and makeup. She opened her door and emerged from the car. She saw Joan walking toward the restaurant.

They were seated and ordered in short time. "Bring me up to speed on Spinder."

"They are really doing a media blitz around this thing. They want to allow cameras in the courtroom," Sophia said. Sophia had gone on CNN to present a rebuttal to Spinder's interview with Larry King two nights earlier. The McBride family was outraged at how public the case had become, but Sophia considered that a naive reaction.

Everything around Spinder was news. He had a reputation on screen for being a bad boy, and this case was one more feather in his cap as far as the media was concerned.

"You've got Judge Malloy, right?" Joan asked.

"Yes. You know he could go either way. I'm not sure what would be better. Spinder's a great actor. I was half believing he should be acquitted."

"I know. I saw him on *Larry King* over the weekend."

"Yeah, I did too."

"Your rebuttal went well." She leaned back in her chair. This was the kind of high-profile case that could make or break an attorney. Sophia knew it and Joan knew it.

"Thanks. What would you do about the media?" Sophia asked.

Joan took a sip of her coffee. Sophia knew her boss and mentor well enough to appreciate the long silences that Joan retreated into sometimes. After a few minutes, Joan lowered her coffee cup.

"I'm not sure. I think you should move to ban the cameras."

"I'll call and have Alice do the paperwork on my way back to the office."

"Good. I've been reading up on Mitch Hollaran. Did you know him at Harvard?"

That was a loaded question. "Yes."

"What's he like?"

"It was ten years ago."

Joan didn't say anything, just waited.

"I think winning is very important to him. I know that he's very thorough. His reputation is enviable."

"Yours is too."

"Thanks."

"All those wins mean only one thing...."

"That he's in for a fall," they both said in unison.

"I'm glad to see you back on track, Sophia. What was the matter with you last week?"

"Hollaran and I had an affair in college," Sophia said.

"Interesting. Will it be a problem for this case?"

"No."

"Are you sure?"

"As sure as I can be, why?"

"I'm going to tell you something that normally I wouldn't."

"Why?"

"I think it might help you."

"Okay."

"When I was about your age I was involved with Maurice Hanner. He and I had a red-hot affair. Going up in front of him in court was torture because of that. For both of us. Eventually he asked me to marry him."

Joan paused and Sophia didn't say anything. Obviously Joan hadn't said yes. She'd often wondered what was in her boss's past but now she knew.

"It wasn't an easy decision. But I don't regret it."

"Is it hard to see him now?"

"Sometimes. But I've made my bed."

Sophia nodded, understanding what her boss didn't have to say. Choices once they were made had to be lived with. She'd done just that when she'd ended her affair with Mitch back at Harvard.

They finished their breakfast and left the restaurant. Sophia's cell phone rang as she was on I-4. There was no voice on the other end, only Stevie Ray Vaughan's guitar. The flush of confidence she'd felt toward her job a minute before changed to confidence that she could handle Mitch. She disconnected the call.

There was a certain truth to knowing your enemy. Though she was honest enough to admit she didn't really know that much about Mitch. Even in college their relationship had been centered around sex and law. She knew he came from California and that he had a brother, but otherwise she knew very little about him.

Talking to Joan this morning she realized she didn't know enough about her adversary. She probably had to do a little more research on him. She picked up her phone and called Alice's voice mail and left a list of things for her secretary to do, including filing the motion to ban cameras in the courtroom and calling the McBrides. The best thing to do with this media circus was to make sure the McBrides presented an united family front to the cameras.

After a few minutes, she picked up her phone again and dialed Mitch's cell phone.

''Hollaran.''

A rush of pleasure tingled through her. It was unexpected and she paused for a moment before pushing those feelings aside. "Morning, Mitch."

"Sophia? What can I do for you this morning?" he asked. He sounded too in control and she decided to play his game. The one he said he wasn't really playing.

"Shake for me."

He laughed and she knew in an instant that he felt what she did. That enthusiasm that came with starting a new case. The energy that came from meeting a lawyer in court who was a worthy opponent. The excitement that came from knowing that their side bet was closer to being realized.

"Are you back in Orlando?" she asked.

"I am. I've set up offices over on Orange Avenue."

"We're filing a motion this morning to ban the cameras."

"We're counter-filing," he said.

It made sense. If Spinder were her client she'd have him on every news program and talk show she could get him on. The man was magic in front of the camera. And from the brief time they'd spent together in the courtroom she knew he had that same charisma in person as well. "I'm not surprised."

"Ready to meet in court?" he asked.

"I'm ready for everything you've got."

She hung up before he could respond. She was

ready to get this case moving forward and ready to prove herself against the man who once made her question herself and her future. And to prove to both of them that she'd made the right choice.

7

SMOKEY'S BLUES HOUSE WAS the kind of bar people went to when they wanted attention. Jason Spinder was the kind of man who was used to being in the middle of the crowd with all eyes on him. Mitch, however, didn't like public scrutiny and was keeping a low profile in the back of the club. You'd never guess from the way Spinder was standing in front of this crowd belting out songs that the young man was nervous about going to trial on Monday.

Mitch wasn't nervous. Sophia had been a worthy opponent up to this point and he knew she'd be just as good when the trial started, but Mitch knew he'd built a solid case. Doubt was all that was required for the jury to acquit Jason.

He was positive that they'd uncovered enough witnesses to inspire doubt in the jury's minds, even though Holly McBride looked like a girl on her way to church. They had pictures of her from the nights leading up to the act with Jason that showed a different side. He'd submitted them as evidence and knew Sophia had seen them. He wondered how she was going to counteract that strong evidence. And he had no doubts that she would.

"Quite a crowd here tonight," Marcus said.

"Not bad. I think I even see some media types."

"You should. I called them all before we left the hotel."

Mitch shook his head. Marcus had worked magic with the press. Jason had been moving through the Orlando night-life scene as though he hadn't a care in the world. Only privately did Mitch and Marcus see the actor sweat.

"Oh, ho, here comes the enemy," Marcus said.

Mitch glanced up to see Sophia moving through the crowd with a group of women. She paused to chat with a local reporter and her smile had a cold edge to it that he knew meant trouble. She then continued on to meet her party at a table halfway across the room from his.

"I wish she weren't so good with the press. Her speech on the steps today made me a little uneasy," Marcus said.

"We'd look like bullies if she wasn't so good."

"That's the truth. Once the trial starts I'm going to pull Jason back and have him show a more serious side."

"Whatever you think is best. I don't need public opinion on my side to win this case."

"I just love it when you say things like that."

Mitch brought his glass to his mouth and drained it in one long swallow. He was drinking ice water tonight. He planned to leave the club in about ten minutes, wanting to review his notes and rehearse his opening comments one more time tonight.

Despite his words to Marcus he knew he needed to be in top form if he was going to beat Sophia in the courtroom. Anything other than a win was intolerable.

He wondered if she'd even noticed him in the back of the room. Probably not. But damn, he noticed her. They'd had little contact outside the courtroom, which seemed the wisest course while they'd both been preparing for a high-profile case, but he'd seen her every night in his dreams.

She'd changed out of the business suit she'd had on earlier today when they'd been at the courthouse for jury selection. Now she wore a short feminine skirt and a lacy shirt.

Jason noticed Sophia and winked at her. "This next song is dedicated to you."

He conferred with the karaoke operator and soon was singing "Man Eater." Sophia laughed and Jason's playful attitude had many in the club laughing with him.

She stood up and took a bow after the song was over. Several of Jason's little fan group booed her. Sophia just smiled at the girls, then walked over to the bar. He watched her move across the room. She had an unconscious grace that had always mesmerized him. The arousal that had been his constant companion since he'd come to Orlando spread throughout his body. He stretched his legs under the table to give his growing erection more room.

Jason finished his set on the karoake machine and Marcus moved off to talk to his client. Jason wasn't much of a singer, but he had charisma and a kind of self-deprecating humor that made him a natural on any mic.

Mitch just sank deeper into his booth and watched Sophia. She must have felt his eyes on her because she glanced up and met his gaze in the mirror behind the bar.

Her lips parted. She paid the bartender and turned from the bar, walking back through the crowded room right toward his table. Damn. He didn't want the press to see them together. But she stopped at her table and dropped off her drink before continuing across the room to the short hallway that led to the rest rooms.

Jason held sway over the press and Mitch decided it was safe to follow Sophia down the dark hallway. What could happen in a very public place with the media so close by? He tossed a few bills on the table to cover the tab Marcus had run.

He adjusted himself under the table before standing. The club was playing a recorded track of popular music but in his head Mitch heard Stevie Ray Vaughan. He entered the hallway. It was empty. At the end of the hall was a door that led outside. Mitch opened the door and stepped out into the balmy Florida summer night.

Sophia was waiting there in the shadows. Her hair curled around her shoulders and when she saw him emerge from the club she stepped forward and took his hand.

A rush of lust engulfed him. God, it had been too long since he'd touched her. He tugged her off balance and wrapped his arms around her. He lowered his mouth to hers. "Hey, man eater."

He cut off her reply with his lips on hers. Pulling gently on her lips, he melded them completely together the way he longed to meld their bodies. He thrust his tongue languidly into her mouth. She made a soft sound in the back of her throat that aroused him to the point of pain.

Her hands held his head as if fearing he'd pull away from her. He wasn't going anywhere. Her tongue swept into his mouth, letting him know she wasn't under his control.

He moved his hands up her head, gripping the back of it and sliding his fingers through her hair. Her hips moved against him. He forced his thigh between hers and bent his leg, lifting her off the ground.

She clung more closely to him. He continued to plunder her mouth, searching for something he knew he'd lost long ago. Something that he was man enough to realize he wasn't going to find in the courtroom facing off against Sophia. Something that he doubted would be assuaged by having her as his love slave for a weekend. Something he realized that he'd never realized he needed until this moment.

And that something was Sophia's complete surrender. He didn't want her in his arms because of a wager. But he'd take her any way he could get her.

SOPHIA WASN'T SURE what she'd hoped to accomplish by luring Mitch out of the club to this private spot. But she did know that she didn't regret this moment. She hadn't had a good night's sleep since he'd sent that tub of Coronas to her and starting tomorrow they'd be seeing each other every day while the trial ran its course.

Fate couldn't be stopped and neither could Mitch Hollaran. His mouth continued to plunder hers. She could do nothing but cling to his broad shoulders and respond to his embrace.

She'd craved him since the last time they'd been together. Every night she'd put on his old T-shirt and had curled up in bed listening to Stevie Ray

Vaughan. She'd remembered the sweet time before she'd made her choice, and the choice and the decisions she'd made haunted her.

His hand molded to the back of her head. His fingers caressing that spot on the back of her neck made shivers spread down her spine. She rocked against the thigh he had between her own.

"Where did this come from?" she asked, breathlessly. "Not that I'm complaining."

One of his hands slid down her back and under the filmy material of her blouse. He lifted his head and stared at her for a long moment, his eyes narrowed, his nostrils flaring and his breath rasping in and out of his wet lips.

"I've been working twelve-hours days trying to forget you but every time I close my eyes..."

He muttered something under his breath that she couldn't make out, then lowered his head to hers once more. This time his kiss was more demanding.

He pulled her lower lip between his teeth and suckled there. She opened her mouth wide and tilted her head to the side, reluctantly it seemed; he let her lower lip free and she teased him with the same caress. His big hand under her shirt circled her back with widening caresses each time coming closer and closer to the edge of her breasts. Finally he touched the side of her right breast, and just teased the bottom side with one long lean finger.

That kiss wasn't the slow seduction he'd been playing at with the gift baskets. This kiss was one from a man pushed past his limits. A man who knew that the end was in sight but couldn't wait another day. She felt the same way.

She was tired of going home to an empty bed and dreaming of him. Tired of pretending that her career was still the only focus in her life. Tired of hiding from the real woman she was, not the woman she'd been content to be.

He dropped openmouthed kisses on her neck, lingering at the base where her pulse beat so strongly. Her nipple pebbled in anticipation of a touch that wasn't coming. She squirmed in his arms, trying to force his touch higher. But he held her still with one hand on her ribs and the other on her hips.

Oh, yes. This is what she'd been secretly waiting for. A man who looked right past the Assistant District Attorney image and saw the woman underneath. The woman who'd been trapped for so long she was almost giddy with the lack of control.

He didn't lift his mouth from her neck and as he continued to suckle there she realized he was leaving a mark on her. Another mark on her, except this one wouldn't be washed away with soap and water.

When he lifted his head she was trembling with need and she knew a quickie in the alley wasn't going to satisfy either one of them. She dipped her head and brushed aside the open collar of his shirt. She bit him lightly at the base of his neck, then suckled him. He tasted slightly salty and uniquely like Mitch.

His hand under her breast moved again, that long finger curling upward and brushing against her nipple. She moaned against his skin.

"Babe, you feel so good in my arms," he said, pulling her head back and kissing her again.

She worked her hands between them and freed the buttons of his shirt. Soon she was caressing the firm muscles of his chest and stomach. His hands didn't stop moving under her blouse, leaving no area of her upper body unexplored.

He pushed her blouse up under her armpits, pulling her forward until they were pressed together. He held her firmly with one hand in the middle of her back. Then he undulated against her like a big cat. She shuddered and held him closer. Loving the feel of him everywhere. They needed someplace where they could get vertical. Someplace where she could let him surround her with all his heat. Someplace like…her house.

The time for games had come to an end and she knew what she had to do. She was close to an orgasm, but didn't want to have another without him inside her.

When he lowered his head and tongued her nipple

she cried out his name. He whispered something against her skin, then treated her other nipple to the same laving.

She let her head fall back. Her own hair brushed the middle of her back, soft and sensuous while his mouth moved on her. Both of his hands were on her hips now and he urged her to rock against his thigh. Unable to stop herself, she did just that, rocking harder and harder until she felt her climax start. Little contractions gave way to greater ones as sensation spread throughout her body. She called out his name and held him closer to her.

He continued to suckle at her breast and move her hips against his thigh until he groaned and she felt his wetness through the fabric of his pants against her thigh.

She cradled him to her. Confident that now Mitch was ready to let go of the past. Ready to put aside the wager they'd made and have a real relationship that involved emotions. And frankly that scared her.

MITCH COULDN'T BELIEVE he'd let this happen. He'd been avoiding her for just this reason. Sophia ran her hands down his back and he knew he should be pushing her away, but instead he wrapped his arms around her and held her tight.

The pale moon cast long shadows in the alley and he was glad for the privacy it provided. It allowed him the freedom to hold her and pretend that this was just another too-vivid dream. Mitch felt as though he was going through a rebirth with Sophia. And he didn't trust it. Didn't trust her.

She smelled so good and felt so right in his arms. He'd known since the day that he'd visited her office that revenge wasn't going to be straightforward. But he could handle the heat. It was the tenderness that surprised him.

He tried to remind himself of all the reasons he shouldn't believe in her tenderness. But, in a startling moment of clarity, he realized that his anger with the way his relationship with Sophia had ended wasn't only directed at her. It was also directed at himself for allowing this woman to see his vulnerabilities and manipulate them.

This time he was stronger. With that thought in mind, he opened his arms and stepped away from her. No matter how right she felt with her head on his chest right over his heart, he knew that soul mate and Sophia Deltonio was an oxymoron.

He smoothed her blouse down and moved away from her. Her lips were full and swollen. Some light spilled out from the club and she carefully avoided that patch of light. She watched him steadily and he sensed her confusion. Maybe with herself, maybe with him. He understood it completely. How could someone who was in essence your enemy make you react so strongly?

For the first time in his life he understood a little of what Dev must go through when he was craving his drug of choice. Because Sophia was in his blood. Only the thought that he had a wager that guaranteed him a weekend of her in his bed was enough to make him let her go tonight.

"Penny for your thoughts," he said, buttoning his own shirt but leaving it untucked. God, he hadn't come in his pants since he'd been sixteen. Why was Sophia the only woman who'd ever made him forget about control?

She shook her head. "All my thoughts involve you, that Stevie Ray Vaughan CD and the Coronas."

"Really?" he asked, surprised she'd admit to thinking about him. But she'd been unflinchingly honest with him this time. He remembered her confession over the phone that he'd collected his pound of flesh. And he wanted to warn her that he wasn't a good guy anymore. That life and experience had worn out any desire he had to play the hero. He was a man who wanted his life back and he wasn't afraid to hurt her if that's what it took.

"Oh, yeah. Come home with me, Mitch. And we can act them out."

"I'm afraid you're going to have to earn that right, babe."

"Earn it in court?"

"That was the deal. Unless you're afraid you can't beat me."

"I'm not afraid of you, Mitch."

"Then I guess we'll have to wait."

He reached out to capture a strand of her hair that the evening breeze blew across her cheek. That curl was soft and bouncy and wrapped around his finger as if it didn't want to let him go. Reluctantly he released her hair and stepped away from her.

"I have an idea."

"What?"

"Let's forget about the past and our wager. And go home and start the affair that's waiting for us."

He was tempted. But the stubborn part of his soul refused to consider her offer. That stubborn man who lived alone in that big Bel Air mansion. That stubborn man who refused to allow the tenderness she called so effortlessly from deep inside him.

He crossed his arms over his chest, leaning back against the wall of the club. The music had started back up again and he could hear Jason inside singing a pop tune with more gusto than talent. Mitch felt the weight of everything he ever wanted and everything he was combine.

Giving up his revenge wasn't something he could

do. It didn't matter how vulnerable Sophia might seem when she was in his arms. She'd taken something from him and he wouldn't have any peace until he'd evened the scales.

"I must decline."

She bit her lower lip and wrapped her arms around her waist, turning away from him. He watched her pull her dignity back around herself. Watched her stand taller, shake her head and when she pivoted back to face him the soft woman he'd held just moments earlier was completely gone.

And he knew that he'd made the right decision as if there were any other one he could make. Sophia Deltonio was a red-hot elixir flowing through his veins and he couldn't compromise his professional integrity by going home with her tonight and by letting her distract him so close to the trial.

He reached into his pocket for his keys and encountered that black velvet ribbon of hers. He caressed it for a second the way he ached to caress her face, to wipe away the pain of his words.

He pushed past the ribbon, palming his keys and pulling them from his pants. "I've got to go."

"You're not ever going to forgive me, are you?"

"Would you be able to forgive that kind of betrayal?" he asked.

She bit her lower lip and watched him with wide

eyes. He wished he could read the emotion there but was half-glad he couldn't.

"See you in court, Hollaran."

She turned and left the alley before he could and he was forced to watch her walk away. Her steps were deliberately slow and her hips moved gracefully with each one. He knew what she was doing. Knew she was aware that he was helplessly watching her. And he knew that she was willing to play by the rules he'd laid down. He regretted the loss of what might have been, but for both their sanity's sake, they needed to focus on the one weekend they had coming. And then, and only then, could the demons of the past be finally put to rest.

8

SOPHIA COUNTED the steps from the courtroom to the bathroom the next day. AC/DC rocked on in her head and she prepared mentally for the jury. She knew her opening remarks backward and forward.

From studying tapes and transcripts of Mitch's past cases she knew what to expect from him. But expecting it wasn't the same as seeing it. She'd seen that determination, charisma and power this morning on the steps of the courthouse when he'd made a few brief remarks to the press.

When they'd stopped her, his words had echoed in her mind and she'd said the only truth she knew. She'd do her best to make sure justice was served.

She'd seen Mitch's mocking grin as he entered the courthouse. She'd taken that grin and used it to temper her determination to win. This was the man she wanted to beat, not the one who'd held her so tenderly last night.

Focusing only on this case she had a moment's clarity as she admitted to herself that her career was no longer the most important thing in her life. Last night on the short drive home, she'd come to understand that she didn't care if Mitch was only after her for revenge. She wanted him anyway.

That didn't say much for her common sense. She entered the handicapped stall in the bathroom. Locked the door behind her and crossed to the mirror over the sink. She braced her hands on the sink and leaned forward, looking into her own eyes and making sure she could see her own conviction there.

Jason Spinder was a Hollywood bad boy who thought celebrity brought him the privilege of behaving on the outside of the law, something that the State and she knew no one had a right to do. She straightened, smiled at herself, knowing when she entered the courtroom, she was entering it to win.

She exited the bathroom and walked back toward the courtroom. Mitch was at the water fountain. She was prepared for his presence today. She was ready to take him on in court and win this case so that she might be able to leave an encounter with him feeling that she was in charge instead of feeling like an aching mass of vulnerability.

Her steps faltered for a second, but then she resumed her determined stride. Counting in the back of her mind, she paused only a second as she passed Mitch, still drinking at the fountain, to pat his butt.

She continued toward the oak doors that held the

arena they'd chosen for their battle. She was suited up and ready to face him.

"Deltonio."

Sophia glanced over her shoulder at Mitch. She tried to tell herself this was a case like any other but as he moved toward her she heard the riffs of Stevie Ray Vaughan and she knew this was like nothing she'd faced before.

"Yes?" she asked.

He stopped a pace away from her and ran his hand down her back, lingering at the curve of her waist. She struggled to keep herself from reacting to his touch. She didn't want to think of Mitch and sex while she was in the courtroom.

"Isn't that the suit you were wearing when I visited you in your office?"

She started to tremble. Oh, God, it was. In one second he'd reduced her from confident career woman to a quivering mass of sexual need. She remembered his hands sliding up under her skirt, his fingers unfastening her buttons and his face as he climaxed over her.

"Is it?" she asked, trying for nonchalance. She'd had the suit cleaned twice because the last time she'd worn it she swore she could still smell Mitch in the fabric. This morning she'd been thinking about the case. This was her opening statement suit.

She'd debated not wearing it, but in the end ritual had won out.

He moved around in front of her. Keeping one hand on her waist. "Yes, it is."

He closed the gap between them. He ran the tip of one finger down the side of her neck, resting it on the love bite he'd given her the night before. He moved his fingertip in a languid circle, made her blood seem to flow heavier and pool in the center of her body.

Damn him. And damn herself for not walking by him. She'd wanted to shake his concentration, and as usual it had backfired.

"I had no idea you had such an eye for fashion." She was really out of her element with him. He made her feel like a first-year law student. She should just walk away. Isn't that what parents and teachers advised kids when they were in a situation that they knew wasn't good for them?

"I'm not interested in fashion, babe. Only in you," he said. She knew he spoke the truth. And a part of her, the silly velvet-ribbon-wearing part, wanted to believe it was because he wanted her as much as she wanted him. But deep inside she knew it was because she was his enemy and that he'd come back into her life for revenge.

"I'd be flattered except that I know you too

well,'' she said, walking away before he could respond.

She didn't pause until she entered the courtroom and took her seat. There were no cameras in the courtroom. She'd won that battle. A courtroom artist sat to one side. Reporters had also been banned. Only Spinder's family and friends and Holly McBride, the seventeen-year-old girl who'd had sex with the twenty-two-year-old actor and her grim-faced parents were in the courtroom.

This case was so delicate and she felt the pressure from the McBride family that she win. She also felt the pressure from her boss, Joan Mueller, who wasn't sure Sophia was really back in the game. Lastly she felt pressure from herself because surrendering to Mitch wasn't something she thought she could do.

THE DAY IN COURT WAS long and invigorating. Mitch knew that winning wasn't going to be easy, but then the things really worth having had always caused him the most work.

Sophia was at the top of her game. She worked the jury with a style and skill he admired, countering each of his witnesses with one of her own and keeping the score even as far as the jury was concerned. She'd changed a lot since their days at Harvard. He wasn't surprised as much as proud.

Pride might not be the right thing for him to feel toward her, but he knew that despite his efforts to keep his emotions from her, it was nearly impossible to do it. She engaged his senses and made him feel alive in a way no other woman had. Seeing her in court and realizing she was his equal here as well... made her irresistible.

Judge Malloy had a reputation for speedy trials. This one, however, was going to play out on its own timetable. Mitch had learned a long time ago not to set his watch or anticipate what a trial would bring. Right now, it was anyone's game and Sophia could win or he could.

The judge dismissed the jury for the day. Sophia left the courtroom without a glance at him. He noticed she took a few minutes to talk to the McBride family and he knew from watching her body language that she was conveying her confidence to them.

Jason too watched the McBrides and Mitch knew from talking to Spinder that he felt a deep sense of betrayal at this case. He'd tried to talk to Holly before the trial had begun but the girl refused to even look at him. Standing next to Jason and watching the women who'd betrayed them both only intensified Mitch's need to win.

Mitch followed Sophia out. The sparring match before they'd entered the courtroom had reminded him that Sophia wasn't a woman who was used to letting anyone get the upper hand. Marcus was waiting for Jason and Mitch lingered when they approached the media who'd been camped out since early morning. He let Marcus and Jason entertain the press on the courthouse steps.

Mitch had found his thoughts drifting to Sophia only twice. Once when she'd tilted her head to the side and watched him during his opening remarks. She'd had the same intense concentration as when she'd held his face in her hands and kissed him. The other time had been when she'd been pacing in front of the jury box and he'd caught a whiff of her perfume.

As soon as he turned it on, Mitch's cell phone beeped with a voice-mail message. Walking to his car, he dialed in to check his messages. The Porsche was hot from sitting all day in the baking Florida sun. He loosened his tie and listened to a stack of messages from his secretary, then froze when he heard Dev's voice on the machine.

During the six weeks Mitch had been in Orlando, Dev had checked into a last-chance rehab center. His voice revealed nothing in the message that simply asked Mitch to call him.

Mitch dialed his childhood friend's number. He'd avoided seeing Dev both times he'd been back in L.A., mostly because he didn't want to face the facts that this time he couldn't bail Dev out. This time Dev had a 24/7 counselor in his pocket. This time Dev was either coming out of rehab and staying clean and sober, or he was going to jail for the next twenty years.

"Devil's Own Breeders," Dev said on the first ring.

"How's the devil?" Mitch asked.

"In hell," Dev said.

"What's going on?" He feared that once again Dev had been picked up for possession or caught driving under the influence. But there were none of the telltale sounds of a jailhouse in the background and his friend was at home.

"Today's confession day," Dev said at last. He sounded tired.

Mitch rubbed the back of his neck, trying to ease his tension. "What do you have to confess to me?"

Dev gave a humorless chuckle. "Nothing, man. You know all my secrets and vices."

"I'm not following."

"I know. I have to call Julie and tell her what's been going on. My counselor says pretending I'm not a user just gives me an excuse to hide my addiction."

"Is your counselor right?" he asked. Dev had been checking in almost every day. Mitch had been there for his friend. But it was hard sometimes to know if that was helping or not. Dev's counselor, Martin Riddel, had advised Mitch to listen to Dev but not to solve his problems.

"Hell, probably. I don't want to do it, Mitch. She's the only good thing that's ever happened to me."

"I know, buddy." A good woman. God knew, Mitch wanted to believe he'd found one long ago. There was a part of him though that believed no such creature existed, and that all men were destined to journey through life searching for her without much success.

"What should I do?" Dev asked.

In the past, Mitch wouldn't have hesitated to give his friend advice. But not today. Coming off the encounter with Sophia, he knew he was in no position to give suggestions to his friend. "I don't exactly have a great track record when it comes to women."

"You do okay with the ladies. You're with someone more than you're alone."

Mitch realized that he'd never really let anyone see his weaknesses. Especially Dev. Maybe Dev needed to know that Mitch had more than his share of failures. "Yeah, but it never lasts."

"You think I should just disappear from her life. That's what my gut says. But my gut also advises me that life is easier when I'm high."

Mitch didn't like to hear his friend talk about his weakness. For most of their adult lives, Mitch had ignored Dev's addiction until Dev got in trouble with the law, then Mitch would bail him out. But this time, Dev's last chance, it seemed important to not ignore it. "Tell her, Dev. If she sticks by you after you confess you'll know you've got someone worth fighting for."

"And if not?"

"Then when I get home we'll go get drunk and curse all women."

"You got women troubles, Golden Boy?"

"Does the devil have hell to pay?"

Dev chuckled and hung up the phone. Mitch leaned back in his seat and watched his trouble-maker leave the courthouse and walk down the street. He watched until she disappeared from sight and wondered just how he was going to get through this trial without surrendering his control and going after her. She'd invited him into her bedroom once and he doubted she'd invite him back again. He was regretting he hadn't taken her up on the invitation when he'd first had the chance.

JOSEPH WAS WAITING in her office when she returned from the courthouse. Sophia was tense and seeing Joseph did nothing to ease the tension. Why was he here? Had Joan decided to add him to the case after all? She had two paralegals working with her and at this late date the addition of Joseph would send a message of fear to the defense.

He wore one of his understated dark-blue suits with a light blue shirt and matching tie. His wardrobe consisted of only shades of blue. When he'd first joined the staff here, he'd been ribbed about it and had told them he liked the blue skies approach to law and thought his suits conveyed that.

But then they all had their little rituals and superstitions, which was why she was worried about his presence here today. She'd had a great day in court though. Only one time had she been distracted by Mitch the man, not Mitch the lawyer. That had been when he'd paced in front of her during his opening remarks. He'd paused to lean on the edge of her table and the scent of his aftershave had assailed her. She'd had to close her eyes for a minute to regain her composure.

Alice was busy on the phone. Sophia dropped the file with notes for her to type in her in-box. She scribbled a Post-it note to let her secretary know she needed the notes before Alice went home.

''Joseph, are you waiting for me?'' she asked.

''I am.''

''Come on in.''

On the credenza was a vase of flowers. She suspected it was from the other ADAs. There were days when she really loved her job.

"I see our flowers arrived," he said, confirming her suspicion.

"Thanks."

"No problem. Listen, I'm going up against Petralucci next week and Joan said you might have some advice."

Sophia sank back in her chair and talked law with Joseph, but her mind was elsewhere. She was afraid the case was too finely matched. Mitch had made some eloquent points in the courtroom and she was regretting the wager she'd made to keep him from realizing how deeply his reappearance in her life was affecting her. Now she feared she might very well lose the case, and even if she didn't, a weekend of sex with Mitch wasn't what she needed, not now while this restlessness was prowling through her soul.

"Deltonio?"

Damn. What had Joseph said? "Sorry, it was a long day. I'm still reviewing it in my head."

"No problem. I've done that a time or two."

"I'll have Alice pull all my notes on Petralucci. He's prone to grandstanding, but otherwise he's a good opponent in the courtroom."

"Thanks," Joseph said, standing to leave.

Sophia followed him to the door. Alice was signing for another basket. "Is this from you guys too?"

"Nope. Just the flowers."

Sophia felt a sinking sensation in the pit of her stomach as Joseph walked over to survey the cellophane wrapped package. Was it from Mitch? The third day they'd had their fantasy day. His fantasy had been her in leather undergarments and high-heeled stilettos. She really hoped he hadn't sent that to her office in a cellophane package.

Joseph chuckled when he looked down at the package and the card taped to it. He winked at her, then walked out without any further comment.

Sophia's feet were stuck to the floor. She couldn't cross the room. She didn't want to see what was waiting for her on Alice's desk.

"Come and see what it is," Alice said with a smile. "It's from Jason Spinder."

Relief flooded through her. Mitch would be in heaven if he knew he'd gotten her without even trying. She badly needed a drink and a good night's sleep that didn't involve vivid erotic dreams.

She walked to Alice's desk and glanced at the package there. A big ceramic popcorn bowl filled with copies of Spinder's recent movies and some microwave popcorn. The note said, *From one fan to another.*

"That man has no shame," Alice said.

"He should. He had sex with an underaged girl."

"I know. He doesn't seem like a sex offender. But he's still so sexy and funny. I've seen all his movies."

"Do you want the basket, Alice?" she asked. Sophia didn't want it. She wasn't keeping any mementos of this case. She knew she'd wear the scars on her soul for a long time to come.

"Really? I'd love it. What's he like in court?"

"He's like any other defendant. Nervous, serious and very aware that celebrity isn't a pass for unlawful behavior."

"You got all that from one day in court?" Alice asked.

Sophia shrugged. Actually, years of practicing law made it easy to read most people and when Jason Spinder stopped acting like the Hollywood bad boy his reputation said he was, he just looked like a really young kid who'd made a mistake and didn't want to go to jail. "I need those notes before I leave. Are there any urgent messages?"

"Two. One from Joan. She wants to see you before you go home. I'll do the notes now so you can take them with you."

"Thanks, Alice. And the second?"

"From Mitch Hollaran regarding the Spinder case. Here's his number."

Sophia took the message slip from Alice and

walked back into her office, closing the door carefully behind her. She sank slowly down into her leather chair and dialed Mitch's number.

"It's Sophia," she said when he answered the phone. "I'm returning your call."

"Wow, that was quick. I just left the message."

"Alice said it was urgent."

"It's not. I just wanted to let you know that I purchased some things for you to wear on our weekend together."

"I hope they fit you because I don't intend to lose."

"They won't fit me. But I'm not worried about taking them back, babe."

"What are you worried about, Mitch?"

"That one weekend won't be enough to get you out of my system."

"Me too," she said and hung up. She didn't need Mitch's call to remind her that she was engaged in a very dangerous game. One she wasn't too likely to win no matter what happened in court.

9

AFTER TEN DAYS Spinder's trial drew to a close. Mitch presented his closing arguments before lunch and Sophia hers after the lunch recess. The jury had been dismissed to deliberate.

"I didn't think I'd be this nervous," Jason said, sitting tensely in the waiting room, looking very much like a twenty-two-year-old kid. And not like a successful multi-million-dollar actor.

"Don't sweat it. Even if they don't go our way, and I believe they will, we'll appeal," Mitch said.

"I don't want to go to jail."

"You won't," he promised. Holly McBride had admitted to using a fake ID to enter the club where she'd met Jason as well as purchasing drinks for herself and Spinder. That was strong evidence that the girl had clearly misrepresented herself as being of legal age. The only thing going against them was the fact that she was a minor and that Jason hadn't asked her if she was of legal age. But Mitch didn't think he would have asked either. Holly looked twenty.

Sophia had presented a strong case. But Mitch had put Jason on the stand and let the charismatic young actor give his testimony. "It's too late now to do anything but hope for the best."

"That's what I like about you, man. You're always honest."

"I learned the hard way that lies don't benefit anyone."

Marcus paced around the waiting room like a nervous beauty queen waiting for an announcement at the Miss America Pageant. "Let's go over your remarks again for the press when we win. I don't want you to appear to be gloating."

"Me either. I just want to put this behind me."

Mitch hoped it would be that easy, but he had the suspicion this case was going to dog Spinder for the rest of his life. The media, and Mitch freely admitted they'd played to the media, didn't forget things like statutory rape.

Mitch excused himself while they worked on Jason's remarks. The hallway outside the courtrooms was empty and he paced down to the end, stopping at the window that overlooked Orange Avenue. It was nearing five o'clock and traffic had started building on the street below.

God, he hoped this didn't go another day. He wanted an end to the waiting. He wanted to know who was going to win the side bet he and Sophia had made. He wanted to have his weekend with her to see if he could really exorcise her from his soul.

He'd optimistically made plans to take Sophia to his parents' condo in Boca Raton. It was a nice place with isolated units and individual porch Jacuzzis. They'd have access to a private beach. If he won, he planned to take his time with her. The orgasms they'd shared had been nice but he wanted to have her in his bed with nothing but time on his hands.

He wanted to once again remind her of everything they'd had together, of how good it had been between them and use the bond of the flesh to bring her once more under his spell. She'd said to him when he'd first arrived in Orlando that she'd been afraid of losing herself. Those words had lingered in the back of his mind. He wouldn't mind if their weekend brought her once again totally under his thrall.

His pager beeped and he glanced down at the alpha-numeric window. The message was simple, asking him and Spinder to return to the courtroom. A verdict had been reached.

He walked slowly back to the conference room and Jason glanced up as he entered. "They're ready for us."

"Isn't that too quick?"

"I don't know."

"What's going to happen when we get in there?" Jason asked.

"The jury will file back in. And then you'll be asked to stand. I'll stand up with you. The judge will ask the jury foreman to read the verdict—don't react to what he says."

"I don't know if I'll be able to do that."

"You're the big bucks actor. I know you can do it," Mitch said.

"Shouldn't we go?" Marcus asked.

"In a minute. I don't want to appear too eager," Mitch studied both men. There was a tension in the room that you could cut with a knife. But strategy was the name of the game and he wasn't going to change his mind.

"Spinder, fix your tie and then we'll leave."

"I've heard they call you Ice Man. Now I know why."

"You haven't seen anything," Mitch said. His Ice Man nickname had started in the days after he'd returned from Massachusetts to California. He'd made up his mind to be ruthless in court, learning to put winning before everything else.

Jason was ready to go and Marcus made a quick call to his office to advise them that the verdict would be returned at any moment.

Mitch reentered the courtroom with anticipation singing in his veins. Whatever the outcome, finally it would mean an end to the sexual tension that had been riding him for the last ten days. Sleep was a distant memory. The only thing he did at night was lie in his bed with tortured dreams of Sophia there with him.

He knew the instant she entered the courtroom. Knew the rhythm of her footsteps as she approached. He leaned back in his seat and studied her as she settled her briefcase on the table in front of her.

She was calm and composed, the essence of a successful lawyer confident of herself and the job she'd done. Mitch had the first niggling of doubt that he might be the loser in today's trial. But when she glanced over at him, then quickly turned away, he felt a resurgence of confidence.

There was nothing to worry over now. They had to wait for the verdict. Whatever the outcome he knew he'd have the answers he'd sought when he'd come east.

He turned to Sophia and gave her the quick once-over. She fidgeted in her chair but met his gaze squarely as he'd suspected she would. He waited a beat, then gave her a wide grin.

SOPHIA TRIED TO RELAX as the verdict was read. It wasn't as if this case was going to make or break her in the D.A.'s office. She'd worked hard for her reputation and one loss wasn't going to ruin it.

She had an impressive record and she'd tried the case the best she could. Even Joan had admitted that putting Spinder on the stand had been a stroke of genius for Mitch.

Jason had dropped the facade of being Hollywood's bad boy and spoke straight from the heart and won over all the female members of the jury. The McBrides were still stern-faced and she knew they'd wanted her to keep the fact that Holly had a fake ID from the trial, but several people had seen Holly with it. Plus Mitch had brought in the guy who'd sold it to Holly.

Sophia thought that if they'd put Holly on the stand they might have won over a few of the jurors, but Holly was no Jason Spinder and the girl was clearly nervous and scared. She'd confessed in a quiet moment to Sophia that she wanted the case to end so she could go back to her normal life.

Why then was Sophia so nervous about the verdict? She wasn't stupid, she knew the weight of the jury's decision had more to do with Mitch than with actually winning the case in her mind.

She'd made her plans for their weekend together, booking a suite at the Ritz-Carlton on Amelia Island. The secluded beach retreat would be perfect for the script she'd written in her head. One of luxury and indulgence. One that was so far removed from her time together with Mitch that she'd never be able to confuse her feelings from then with her feelings for Mitch now. And she reminded herself firmly, her feelings for Mitch were no more than lust.

Deliberately, she leaned back in her chair as the judge bid Spinder to stand. She was acutely aware of Mitch standing alongside his client.

This was the part of her job she liked least. This waiting to hear. There was nothing more she could do at this point. A knot of nerves made her feel sick to her stomach.

She held her breath as the judge asked for the jury's decision. The foreman, an elderly grandfather who had been one of her choices on the jury, handed the decision to the bailiff who took it to the judge. He glanced at the paper, then asked the jurors to stand and affirm that this decision was theirs. Finally, the foreman announced the decision. "Not guilty."

Blood rushed through her body. She gripped the edge of the table in front of her. Oh…my…God.

The trial concluded. She was aware of the judge thanking the jury for their work. Very aware of the McBrides, too—Holly wasn't crying and Sophia could see something akin to relief in her eyes. Stanley McBride, Holly's father, looked angry and

Sophia was afraid she was going to have to keep a close eye on him.

Focusing on the McBrides gave her an excuse to ignore the fact that she'd just lost a very serious bet.

She felt frozen. She'd counted on being in control of Mitch. She'd counted on having the freedom to set the pace and hide her true emotions. She'd counted on the charmed life she'd always lived continuing.

She gathered her papers together. Spinder stopped by her table, giving her that million-dollar grin. "Guess you'll have to find another man."

"Guess so. You stay out of trouble. Next time luck might not be on your side."

He flashed her another grin and sauntered out of the courtroom.

Sophia went to the McBrides. "We can file an appeal first thing in the morning."

"Yes, I want you to start doing that," Stanley said.

"No," said Holly. "I don't want to go through this again."

The two looked as though they were going to argue it out in the courtroom. "Talk it over at home and call my office tomorrow."

Mrs. McBride nodded and slid her arms through her husband's and daughter's and led them out of the courtroom. Slowly the room emptied leaving

Sophia alone with Mitch. She thought about doing something childish like refusing to look at him or what her gut really wanted her to do, punch him in the nose.

"Don't gloat," she warned when he stopped next to her.

"I'd never dream of it."

She glanced up at him. She'd envisioned this moment many times. And every time she'd pictured it, she'd been standing over him filled with power and flushed with victory.

"You gave it your best shot," he said.

"Yes, I know. Good game and all that," she said, glancing down at her watch. She had nothing scheduled tonight but needed to escape. "I've got to go."

"Don't let me keep you," he said.

"I won't." She stood and started to walk out of the courtroom. Mitch kept pace with her. She pretended she wasn't aware of him. Wasn't aware of his heat and his scent. Wasn't aware that she'd given this man the right to do whatever he wanted with her body.

"Sophia," he said, stopping. She paused but didn't turn to face him. Though she knew better than to give ground, sometimes it was easier to not face the enemy, and the last few weeks had proven without a doubt that Mitch was her enemy.

Her intimate enemy.

He paced around in front her, shifting his briefcase to his left hand and tilting her head back so that their eyes met.

"If you've changed your mind, I won't hold you to your word."

Did he mean it? She almost took him up on the offer but in the end she couldn't. She needed closure with Mitch. "I don't welsh on bets."

He studied her face for a long minute, then rubbed his finger against her cheek before dropping his hand. "I'm glad. I'll pick you up on Friday afternoon. Give me your address."

She took out one of her business cards and wrote her home address on the back of it. "Do you need directions?"

"I'll call if I do."

"What should I pack?" she asked. She had no idea where he'd take her for the weekend. "Are we going to your hotel?"

"No, we're going to Boca Raton. Just bring the gifts I sent you. I'll provide everything else you'll need."

"Mitch, I'm…"

"Yes?"

"I'm not sure how good a slave I'll be. It's been a long time since I let a man tell me what to do."

He tilted his head to the side, studying her. She wondered what he was thinking, then admitted to herself she probably didn't want to know. For the first time since she'd made the wager she thought about the reasons why Mitch wanted her to be his sex slave for a weekend, and none of them were comforting.

"Then I'd say you're overdue."

"I'm serious, Mitch."

"I am too. I know how to make you obey."

That was exactly what she'd been afraid of. Her worst fears were going to be realized and there was nothing she could do to stop it. She'd given her word. She had in fact been the one to bring up the bet. She'd been so confident of a win she hadn't contemplated the consequences of what she'd done until this moment.

Neither of them said a word but they both knew he was the last man to make her obey. The last man she'd wanted to please. The last man she wanted to know that she still had so much insecurity.

MITCH LEFT THE BAR a little after ten. Spinder's celebration would more than likely continue until the wee hours of the morning. But Mitch had a very different celebration in mind. One that involved him and the sexy district attorney from his past.

He'd sent her another gift, this one from the third day of their long-ago vacation. They'd called it their fantasy day. His fantasy had been Sophia decked out in leather and a pair of very spiky stiletto heels. Her fantasy had been him bare chested, reading Shakespeare by a crackling fire. So he'd sent her a small leather-bound volume of sonnets. He wondered what she'd thought when she opened it up.

He'd been tempted to call her but knew that anticipation was a powerful tool. Anything he said or did would probably dull in comparison to whatever she feared he'd do. But revenge wasn't as satisfying as talking to Sophia, as sparring with her and learning all over why he'd fallen in love with her in the first place.

He rubbed the back of his neck. He was in control this time. He'd learned enough from the past to never again let himself be defenseless with Sophia.

He fished her business card out of his wallet and dialed the home number she'd written on the back. She answered on the first ring.

"Hello?" she said, her voice not at all husky or sleepy.

"It's me," he said.

"Mitch," she said. Just his name but there was a wealth of unanswered emotions in her voice. It wasn't that late.

"What are you doing?" he asked.

"Hmm…I have to wonder why you're calling, Mitch? Hoping I'm sitting here stewing over your win?"

Knowing he'd won, he couldn't wait to claim his prize. But he wasn't about to tell her that.

"Are you?" he asked, leaning back in the seat of his car. The parking lot was dark; only one streetlight on the other side of the lot worked. He closed his eyes and imagined Sophia in her home. Once again he wondered what it looked like.

"What do you think?" she asked, a teasing lilt in her voice.

"I think yes. You're sitting on your bed, wearing some sexy lingerie and thinking of me."

"Ha."

"Am I right?"

"Maybe."

"Come on, babe. You can admit it."

"I'm not admitting anything to you," she said, again with that flirty quality.

But he knew that she was telling the truth. She'd reiterated what he already knew. The bet, this weekend wasn't about anything other than sex for her and some sort of retribution from the past for him. It was the chance for him to leave on his own terms and not because she'd betrayed him.

"Mitch, you still there?" she asked.

This time he heard the rustle of sheets and the creak of the bedsprings. *She was in bed.*

What was she wearing? "Yeah, I'm here. Did you get my gift?"

"I did. Thank you. It's a beautiful book."

"You're welcome." He'd picked it up four years ago when he'd been in London on vacation. He'd had no plans at the time to ever see Sophia again but he'd bought it anyway. He'd also bought her a French silk peignoir, which was already in the suitcase he'd packed for her.

Silence buzzed on the open line and he could hear her breathing. Unbidden he remembered the night before the trial and the feel of her in his arms. The brush of her breath against his skin. He imagined he heard the rustle of a silk negligee against her smooth skin.

"What do you have planned for this weekend?" she asked at last.

Her tied to his bed for two days, his cock said. But the part of him that hungered for revenge had a different sort of thing in mind. And Mitch knew he was playing a dangerous game because his object was to bring Sophia back under his spell. And to do that he'd have to risk falling for her again. "It's a surprise."

She made a tsking sound. "You can tell me, counselor."

"Would you have told me?"

"We'll never know," she said.

"Why did you make this bet, Sophia?" he asked. That was the one thing he couldn't figure out. It didn't fit with the woman he'd come to know in the courtroom the last ten days.

"I don't know," she said in a quiet voice.

"I'm glad you did."

"You're just saying that because you won."

"Probably," he admitted.

She laughed, and his heart ached a little at the sound. Her happiness didn't depend on him, didn't matter to him but for a moment he wished it did.

"What were you planning if you'd won?" he asked.

"Why, need some help?"

"The day I can't figure out what to do with a beautiful woman who's my love slave will be a sad one. I'm just curious about you."

"Curious how?"

"About your fantasies."

"What makes you think they've changed?"

He knew they had because the woman he remembered had developed into a sophisticated and successful lady. Surely, her fantasies where men were concerned had developed as well. "Well you've changed."

She sighed. "Not that much. Good night, Mitch."

"Night, Sophia," he said, disconnecting the call. He turned on his car and drove back to his hotel. He reminded himself that his quest for vengeance had finally borne fruit and soon Sophia Deltonio would be out of his system. Somehow it didn't feel as good as he'd always imagined it would be.

10

JOAN'S OFFICE WAS a little bit chilly when Sophia entered it on Friday. She'd been trying to ignore Mitch all day and even though he hadn't set foot in her office today, he dominated the space. Her pager vibrated and she glanced down at the alpha-numeric display area.

Six hours until you are mine.

A purely sexual thrill shot through her body. She shivered a little as she sat in the guest chair in her boss's office waiting to be admitted into the inner office.

She had six hours left until she and Mitch would leave for their weekend together. Six hours until he showed up at her door and took over her life. Six hours until she'd have to surrender her will and submit to his.

With each communication from him either via her pager or her voice mail she felt the chains around her tightening. She wanted to run. She wanted to hide and escape from him. Yet at the same time she couldn't control the excitement flowing through her veins.

She could let go of her control. In fact, their bet guaranteed she'd bow to his will, and deep inside she rejoiced.

But right now she had to concentrate on her job. Her vacation was due to start on Monday. Sophia had debated since Wednesday the wisdom of taking a vacation after her weekend with Mitch. Would it give her too much time to think? Very much afraid that it would, she'd thought about going to visit her folks in Arizona, but in the end hadn't called them.

She had Alice making copies of all the pending cases so that Sophia could take the files home with her and work during her vacation. There was still a restlessness in her soul that her work couldn't tame, but she wouldn't let Mitch dominate her vacation time.

Kyle Martin, Joan's secretary, announced Sophia. She entered her boss's office and took a seat. Joan's office walls were covered in awards and photos of the District Attorney with prominent citizens. Sophia studied them, envisioning them on her wall and for once didn't get the same rush of satisfaction she usually did.

"Thanks for coming right down, Sophia."

"No problem."

Joan shuffled through some papers on her desk.

"I wanted to let you know that we've made a decision on the Deputy District Attorney opening."

Sophia felt as if all the air had been sucked from the room. She tried to keep up the facade of nonchalance but had the feeling she was failing miserably.

"We want you in that position," Joan said.

Yes, she thought. "Great. I'll cancel my vacation and start on Monday."

"Not so fast. I don't want you to accept this position yet," Joan said. "Take your vacation and make sure this is what you want."

Dammit. She should never have mentioned Mitch to her boss. "We've been over this. I want the job."

"I'm not backing down on this. You haven't had any time off for the last five years."

She didn't want to take time off now. Her goal was in sight. She'd almost forgotten how hard she'd worked for this moment. "You're right."

Joan nodded, jotting a few notes on the pad in front of her. "Good. Leave your contact numbers with Kyle. Are you ready for your vacation?"

"Yes. It's going to be hard to take the time off."

"Believe me, I know. But when you come back you'll be ready to get back in court and win again."

Sophia remembered Joan telling her about the affair she'd had with Judge Hanner. She knew then that her boss had chosen between a man and the

D.A.'s office. And the office had won. Sophia always thought she'd make the same choice, but now she wasn't so sure.

Her boss had just given her the one thing she'd been working toward. Sophia was excited but that excitement dulled when compared to Mitch.

"You're right. I'm taking my notes on the Markingham case with me."

"Sophia?"

"Yes?"

"Leave your work here."

"I'd rather not."

"Trust me on this. You need a complete break. I want you back here refreshed and refocused."

Refocused. What did Joan mean? Had she sensed that she'd stopped thinking about law 24/7? Had she somehow guessed that her nights were filled not with reruns of the previous day's time in court but with one lawyer? Did she know that the law, though always fascinating, paled in comparison to Mitch?

"I have been focused," she said, but she knew she hadn't been. Oh, God, what was happening to her? She knew she should have gotten out of town the moment she saw that damned Corona basket tied with a black velvet ribbon.

"You have, but then you haven't. It's like you're going through the motions of being who I expect you to be here."

"I'm not. I know what I want."

"What is that?" Joan asked.

"The Deputy D.A. spot."

"When you return in two weeks, we'll talk about it."

Sophia knew she was being dismissed and she stood and left the office. Walking back to her own she made an important decision. She was going to take that new job and she was going to mirror her life after her boss's. But first she was going to indulge the woman she'd been hiding since she'd left Harvard. The woman who had a very sensual nature and a very vivid imagination. That woman had gone into hiding because she wasn't one who could focus on a career when the man who enflamed her senses was nearby.

MITCH DROVE to his parents' condo on the beach on Thursday and set up everything the way he wanted it. He'd cleared out one of the smaller bedrooms and set it up similarly to their college apartment. They'd lived in a studio with a small kitchenette.

With a buzz of anticipation zipping through his veins, he pulled to a stop in front of Sophia's house at precisely 6:30 on Friday evening. Taking a deep breath, he reminded himself that he wanted to get to the beach house before he started his conquest of her body.

Frankly, he didn't think he'd be able to make it that long. He'd had the most lurid dream about her last night, and it had been tinged with a desperation he didn't like feeling. He knew his hold on her was fragile, that it had always been very tenuous. He hoped that vengeance was a good enough shield against the emotion she called from him with an effortless ease that made him feel like her puppet.

He was hard just thinking of the fact that Sophia had pledged herself to him for this weekend. She'd promised that she'd be his completely and his gut instinct was to toss her over his shoulder and carry her off someplace dark and quiet where he could stake his claim.

He'd expected one of those high-rise condos but her place was homey. It was a cute little town house with a garden out front and a wreath on the door.

He parked the car and sat there for a minute adding this new piece to the puzzle that was Sophia. He remembered every detail of their time together and realized they'd never discussed the future, never once discussed what kind of house they'd live in, what kind of family they'd wanted. What type of life they might have together.

He knew little about her background, only that she'd been the cosseted youngest child. She was the only girl in a very male-dominated Italian-American family. But what made her tick he'd never tried to understand.

For the first time he doubted himself and his quest for revenge. How could she have known that he wanted her to be his wife when he'd never let the subject come up? He knew he'd hidden what he'd been feeling from her. She'd made everything too intense and he'd done the only thing he'd been able to. Pretend their relationship was normal instead of out of this world.

New discoveries or not Sophia was his for the weekend and he intended to take full advantage of the situation.

He rang her doorbell, heard her footsteps, and then she opened the door. A gush of cool air greeted him.

"Come in," she said. Her hair was damp and she smelled fresh and clean. He wanted to muss her up, to make her sweat and erase the fragrance she wore with the natural scent of the woman underneath.

He stepped over the threshold. There was a deacon's bench in the foyer with a small valise sitting on it. Her purse was next to it along with a pair of large sunglasses and a straw hat.

There was no nervous shifting or shyness in Sophia at this moment. She wore a slim-fitting red sundress that ended mid-thigh. The scooped neckline exposed the tanned tops of her breasts. Her hair hung free, curling around her neck and shoulders.

"I packed a few things," she said, gesturing to the case. He remembered Sophia liked to travel light and wasn't surprised by her small bag. What surprised him was the lack of a food bag. Sophia had always packed snacks for their road trips that would have made a gourmand envious.

"The CDs I sent?" he asked, looking around but not seeing anything resembling a cooler.

"Yes, a few other items in case you get tired of being the boss."

That brought his attention off food and firmly back to the woman in front of him. He had every detail of their weekend planned. Surrendering control to her for even a short amount of time wasn't going to happen. The last time he'd let his guard down around her he'd taken a hit that he was still recovering from. "I doubt that'll happen."

"I don't. You like aggressive women," she said with a sly grin that went straight to his groin. It surprised him how much she remembered about him. It shouldn't though; he knew that she had the same knowledge about him that he had about her. Still, every time she used that knowledge, he felt edgy and excited in a purely sexual way.

"Not anymore."

"Really?" She tilted her head to the side. She

closed the small gap between them in two very short steps, then grasped the back of his neck and tugged his head down to hers. She took his mouth in a kiss that made him harden. He was too full—about to burst. She stood on tiptoe, caged his head in her hands and held him still while she took the kiss she wanted.

God, she was right. He did like aggressive women.

"It's not too late to change your mind, Mitch."

"About?" he asked, trying to sound normal when all he wanted to do was push her up against the wall and thrust into her body.

She rubbed his lower lip with her thumb. "About who gets to be master."

"Babe, that was nice. But I like what I have planned much better."

"Suit yourself," she said, stepping around him to pick up her hat and glasses.

"I intend to."

"If you get that bag, I've got a cooler in the kitchen."

"Not so fast. From this moment forward, you're mine."

"Okay. Do you want to get the cooler?" she asked.

"This isn't about the luggage. This is about our agreement."

She said nothing, only stared at him and he noted for the first time the hint of nervousness in her eyes. He wondered what her ballsy play to get him to change his mind had really been about.

"I'm waiting, Sophia."

"For what?"

"For your agreement."

She sighed. "From this moment on I'm yours."

He shoved his hand into his pocket and found the velvet ribbon he'd been carrying around for too many years. "Until Sunday evening when I drop you back off here, right?"

"Yes, Mitch. Now can we go?"

"Not yet. Turn around."

She did so slowly. He lifted her hair from the back of her neck and leaned down. Brushing his lips against her neck he watched her body react as gooseflesh appeared and spread down her arms. He knew if he slid his hands to her breasts he'd find her nipples hardening. Not yet, he thought.

"Hold your hair up," he said.

She did as he'd ordered. He took the velvet ribbon from his pocket and wrapped around her neck. It fastened in the back with a snap that Sophia had sewn herself years ago in their apartment. He'd watched her make the ribbon and then wear it.

"Drop your hair," he said.

She did. She stood frozen in her foyer. Her hand at her neck. Her head bowed.

"Turn around, Sophia."

She did so slowly, and when she faced him, he saw something in her eyes he hadn't expected to see. A deep emotion that warned him that walking away from her this time was going to be harder than he imagined.

MITCH'S TURBO PORSCHE was a convertible and he put the top down after leaving her house. It was August and hot and she was more than ready for fall. But that season was a long time from coming to Florida. Sweat formed on the back of her neck as they drove through her development and out to I-4.

Even though she knew the car was a rental, it suited Mitch. He had a local rock station playing on the radio. He took her hand, resting it on his thigh. She stroked his leg, reaching between his legs to his hardening erection.

"I don't remember saying you could touch me," he said, in an incredibly arrogant way.

"I don't remember asking," she returned, scraping her fingernail down his zipper.

He sucked in a breath and immediately she felt him harden under her fingers. She tilted her head to the side to give herself a better view of him.

But he placed his hand over hers and held it in

place. He didn't have to say the words *I'm in charge*
but it was understood. She felt the force of his will
and knew that she had to find a way to protect herself from him. Sex with other men had never
touched her as deeply as sex with Mitch. She leaned
her head back against the seat, closing her eyes. But
all she could do was feel his mouth on the back of
her neck, his muscled thigh under her fingers and
the sweat dripping down the back of her neck.

His cell phone rang and he let go of her hand to
answer it. She immediately went back to stroking
his leg with her fingers, edging nearer and nearer his
groin.

"Hollaran," he said into the phone. His voice was
strong and powerful, much like the man himself.

She grasped the tab of his zipper and pulled it
down far enough to slip her forefinger inside. Mitch
wasn't wearing any underwear. She caressed the
burgeoning head of his cock. His skin was satiny to
her touch and very hot.

The knowledge that she'd aroused him made her
squirm in her seat. She spread her fingers, widening
the gap of his zipper, intent on taking his length in
her hands, but Mitch stopped her. He held her hand
palm open over his exposed flesh. He covered the
speaker of his phone and turned to her with eyes
that promised retribution.

"Enough."

He listened for a few minutes. "Okay, Dev. Call me after you talk to her."

Mitch disconnected the call. He lifted her hand back to his thigh and gingerly refastened his pants.

"Too much?"

"Not quite. But since you're eager to get things started…"

"Yes?"

"Are you wearing panties?"

She nodded.

"Take them off."

The traffic was heavy on the interstate and the chance of discovery excited her.

She put both hands on her thighs and started to slide them up her legs.

"Slowly, babe. I want to enjoy this."

She did as he asked, slowly edging the fabric of her skirt up her thighs. Her skirt was made of a cool rayon material that felt good against her skin. She leaned her head back against the leather car seat and faced him. He slowed the car as traffic built to a jam. Mitch smiled at the elderly couple in the car next to them and then raised both eyebrows at her.

"I'm waiting."

She rubbed her legs and watched his eyes track the movement. "You told me to take my time."

"Indeed I did."

The skirt slid to her upper thigh and traffic moved

forward again, this time at a moderate speed. Mitch kept one hand on the wheel and used his right hand to lift her skirt to her waist.

Her underwear had been hand-made in France. She bought them off the Internet. He groaned. She took the sides of the panties and pushed them down her thighs and over her knees.

"Push your skirt down," Mitch said. His hand remained where it was high on her thigh.

His big fingers spread out until the tip of one of them rested very near her clitoris. He slowed the car again as the traffic grew slower. Though she was covered modestly now, the knowledge that she was sitting bare-assed with her lover's hand on her thigh was enough to make moisture pool between her legs. She shifted in her seat. Mitch's fingers slid forward, he slipped one inside her, encountering the wetness there.

"No need to ask if you like it," he said. "Put your hand back on my thigh."

"I don't think this is a good idea."

"I do," he said, in that firm voice again.

She did as he asked her to, her hand resting low on the inside of his thigh.

They didn't speak for the next ten minutes as they moved slowly through the traffic. He wedged one finger into her body and just let it rest there. She felt edgy and ached for his possession.

"Who was that on the phone?" she asked.

"A friend," he answered at length, pushing his finger deeper inside her. She tightened around him, trying to pull him deeper. He retreated, taking his finger from her and placing it on her thigh.

"Oh, you have friends?" she asked. She hated this. Never again was she giving a man rights to her body. She slipped her hand higher once again, and rubbed him through his pants.

He glanced over at her and then lifted his hand from her leg and touched the ribbon at her neck. His hands were slightly damp and sticky from her body. "Remember what I said."

"I told you I wouldn't be any good at this. I'm not used to taking orders."

"Do you want me to punish you?" he asked.

Her pulse jumped through the roof at the suggestion. She didn't answer.

"Very well. When we arrive at the beach house I'll see to it."

"Mitch—"

"Yes?" he asked in that brash way of his.

She knew anything she said right then would just add to the flames already running rampant in her body. "Nothing."

"That's what I thought. You're a quick learner."

"Yes, I am. But I don't like to lose."

"Why does this have to be about losing? We both

want each other. We both like playing games. That's all this is.''

''I can't forget that you're out for revenge and I don't want…''

''I'm not going to hurt you, Sophia. Even though I'd originally planned to.''

''What made you change your mind?''

''Nothing.''

''Come on, Mitch. I'm sitting here butt-naked awaiting some sort of punishment you're going to dole out. I think the least you can do is come clean.''

''Butt-naked? I thought it was buck-naked.''

''Either way. Tell me why you changed your mind.''

''I can't say for sure. I think it had something to do with what you said about me already having my pound of flesh.''

''So you don't want it anymore?''

''No, there's a part of me that still wants it. But there is also…a part of me that wants to believe the Hollaran family legend.''

''What legend?''

''That true love comes just once.''

''Do you think I'm your true love?''

''Not unless I'm a closet masochist.''

His words hurt but she understood what he meant. Even now she still wasn't willing to put any man first. Not even Mitch. ''What's the Hollaran family legend?''

''You'll love this. Men in our family traditionally find their mate in college and marry only once.''

She pulled her hand back into her own lap and stared at Mitch. Oh, please, she thought. Don't let Mitch have believed I was his one true love. Because if he had he'd never forgive her and a pound of flesh wasn't going to satisfy him. He was going to want to destroy her life the way she must have destroyed his.

11

"DID YOU BELIEVE the family legend, Mitch?" Sophia asked quietly after a few minutes had gone by.

The scenery in Florida was so different from California. Lush green marshes lined the road and Mitch had the feeling here that man was still fighting the battle to keep nature from encroaching. He was fighting a battle too, to remember he was here for revenge.

She used the same tone of voice she'd used in the courtroom, and Mitch shook his head. He wasn't some damned reluctant witness on the stand. He was a man with a plan, and revealing all to Sophia wasn't part of it.

Mitch concentrated on the road ahead, ignoring the woman next to him. But inside he knew the truth. Hell, yeah, he'd believed it up to the moment she'd ripped his heart out and left him feeling like a fool. But he was in control this weekend, not Sophia, and he had no intention of sharing that with her.

Sophia Deltonio was a man eater and she'd cut

her teeth on him. This time he was the one planning to do the eating. He thought of where he'd start and his mood lightened.

"What do you think?" he said at last. He wasn't sure how they'd bungled onto this conversation. He only knew he had to get them away from the one subject he didn't want to discuss with any woman— especially Sophia.

She shrugged. The scrap of fabric that passed as a strap on her dress slid, the movement revealing clean smooth skin unmarred by a bra strap. "I'm not sure. I hope you didn't believe that..."

Focus on sex. It was the one thing he knew how to control around Sophia. Actually he didn't really know how to control it. He expected certain reactions from himself and from her and those at least were manageable. He reached between the seats to the cooler wedged behind Sophia's seat. "Why not?"

"Because if you did...then I hurt you far worse than I ever knew I could."

He pushed the lid off the cooler and felt around for a chunk of ice. Just what he needed. "Well, you didn't."

"Are you sure that isn't what this weekend and all those gift baskets were about?" she asked.

"All about what?" The baskets were his way of making sure she had some emotional investment in him. His way of tying the woman she was today to the woman she'd been in the past. His way of making his vengeance just a little sweeter.

"Revenge?" she asked.

He refused to lie to Sophia. One of the reasons why he felt justified for his actions was the fact that he'd never deceived her. "Would you want revenge?"

"I might. But then men have been using women for centuries without retribution."

Sophia had always been a strong feminist, and her mentors had encouraged that independent spirit. Having been raised by a very liberal mother, Mitch had been on her side and supported her attitude. "Is that what you thought I was doing? Using you?"

"Were you?" she asked, pining him with her Pacific Ocean blue gaze.

Honestly, he wasn't sure. "Not intentionally."

"That's what I figured." She gave him a half smile, then looked away.

What did that mean? "Is that why you did it? For womankind?"

"No. I did it for me. And for you. We were too young to be that intense."

"It's only when you're young that it seems intense."

"So you don't feel for me now what you used to

feel?'' she asked, placing her hand on his thigh again. His cock twitched. ''Mitch?''

There was a loaded question, he thought. Time for the distraction.

He lifted his hand from the cooler and ran the ice cube down the side of her neck, coming to rest on the very back of her neck. Shivers raced through her body and he forced himself to keep his eyes on the road until they passed a minivan. Then he glanced over at her. She sat still, her hands clenched in her lap, her nipples tenting the fabric of her blouse.

''What were we talking about?'' he asked, finally feeling he'd regained the upper hand.

''I'm not sure,'' she said. Condensation from the ice cube slid down her back and she squirmed a little.

''Too cold?'' he asked, sliding the melting cube back and forth along her skin. She trembled under his touch.

She shifted away. He took the remaining bit of ice and put it in his mouth, then reached for the velvet ribbon around her neck, and he rubbed the edge of it with his cold finger.

''Sophia?''

''Yes?''

''Answer me.''

He saw her struggle for the first time since he'd walked back into her life to conceal her reactions to him, and he realized that maybe revenge wasn't going to be that hard to get. A part of his soul wanted to warn her not to trust him. But he knew Sophia Deltonio didn't trust any man.

"No," she said at last.

He grabbed another cube from the cooler behind her seat and this time, he slid it along the side of her face and down the side of her neck. He held the melting ice against her skin and watched as the water snaked slowly down her chest disappearing into the bodice of her dress.

She rotated her shoulders against the seat. He didn't know if she was trying to escape the icy drip or direct it. He took his eyes from Sophia and checked the road. Their turn was coming up. He rubbed the cube over her lips and then slipped it inside.

She was quiet as he exited the interstate. When he pulled to a stop in the garage under his parents' condo he turned to her and smiled. "Now the fun begins."

SOPHIA WAS ENERVATED from the conversation with Mitch. She tried to pretend he was Robert, the man who'd asked her to marry him or another faceless man she was just going away with to have mindless sex with. But her heart reminded her this was Mitch

Hollaran. The only man who'd ever made her question her loyalty to her career.

She exited the car without waiting for him to open her door. She needed to escape. She knew she'd given her word. She'd made promises and she intended to keep them, but she had to regain some of her control. She needed to take a few minutes to find her safe place and tuck the emotions he'd called so effortlessly back away.

She grabbed her purse. Mitch popped the trunk and tossed her the keys. "Go upstairs. I'll be up in a minute."

She nodded and walked sedately toward the garage door leading to the house. She wanted to run. Unlocking it, she paused to glance over her shoulder at him and smile sweetly before disappearing inside the house. She climbed the carpeted stairs quickly and stopped at the top.

The condo was nice and cool. A living room opened into a dining area with large windows and a small kitchen. There was a short hallway that she guessed led to the bedrooms and a glass door that led to a balcony.

She slipped off her shoes and dropped her purse on the couch before opening the door and stepping outside. The sun was already setting and she watched the ocean waves break on the shore, the waves' relentless cycling mirroring her feelings. No matter how far she ran she always washed back up on the shore that was her and Mitch.

She fingered the velvet ribbon around her neck. She couldn't believe he'd kept it all this time. She braced her arms against the iron railings, leaning against them. She searched the horizon for answers to the questions buzzing through her, but she knew there weren't any. The only answers she'd find were hidden even from herself and that she'd hoped, prayed that no man would ever make her acknowledge again.

But Mitch had brought that all to the foreground with one simple sentence. One taste of his past. That tempted her with what might have been her future. True love. God, she'd never really dwelled on love. Not since she realized that Mitch was either going to have to leave her life or she'd never become a lawyer.

She'd done more than send him on a false trail. She'd gone to her mentor and made Mitch sound incompetent. Then she'd sat back and let those two lies destroy what would have been the beginning of a promising law career.

The ocean breeze was warm and gentle and on the beach below she saw a couple holding hands and walking. Her heart ached at the thought of never having that. Never finding a person she connected with so deeply and so safely that it didn't matter if she lost her soul in him because he'd show her how to find it again.

It was easy to forget those girlhood dreams she'd had of finding her perfect mate. She lived away from her family and her friends—the few she had were all career driven like her. They'd get together and talk about the freedom they had, the choices they'd made, and never lamented the lack of a spouse or children. But sometimes in the night when she was all alone, she did miss those things and she wanted something she was afraid to vocalize.

She heard the door open and Mitch's footsteps on the stairs. She wasn't ready to face him again but knew she had better make herself. She took a deep breath and walked back into the condo meeting him at the top of the stairs.

"Want some help?" she asked. He was loaded down with bags and carrying the cooler. Big and strong with a sheen of sweat on his brow, Mitch looked too tempting. This was the man she wanted to have an affair with. Too bad he was watching her with that cold gray gaze of his that made her feel he saw straight past her defenses.

"I've got it."

Unable to resist herself, she squeezed his biceps where it was flexed from carrying his load. He froze, exhaling in a rush. "You sure do, macho man."

He gave her an exasperated look and she wondered at the wisdom of tormenting the man she'd given complete power over her body.

Fear made her reckless and that look in Mitch's eyes made her want to push him hard so that he'd get whatever he had in mind over with. "So you want me naked on the couch?"

"When was I ever so...obvious?"

Never. Mitch wasn't one of those bragging, swaggering guys. He'd always had to set the stage and take his time. She'd never complained. He was a very thorough lover and she knew whatever he had planned would satisfy her completely.

He set everything down in the middle of the floor. "I've got to make one more trip to get the rest of your goodies. I left a bottle of wine in the fridge chilling. Why don't you open it up and grab a couple of glasses for us."

"When were you here?" she asked.

"Yesterday. I wanted to make sure everything was in place for you."

He turned toward the stairs and pivoted so she didn't have to watch him leave. She entered the small kitchen. It was done in a cheery yellow with bright white daisies as the border. The kitchen also had a door leading to the balcony.

She found a bottle of Chardonnay chilling in the fridge. The corkscrew was sitting on the counter next to two wineglasses. She found a tray of cheese and fruit in the fridge and set them on the wrought-iron table on the balcony.

She opened the wine with no struggle. She'd lived alone long enough that she'd learned to open her own bottles. She didn't dwell on that too long, picking up the glasses and carrying them along with the Chardonnay outside. She poured some in each glass.

Fleetingly she thought of tipping the bottle to her lips and getting a buzz going so that she could concentrate on the pleasant feelings it elicited and not the raucous ones that Mitch brought to the surface. She had a feeling that not even getting blind drunk was going to help.

MITCH BROUGHT the last of the bags up the stairs. He could see Sophia's legs propped on the banister. To the world, she looked cool and composed. If only he hadn't seen her lips trembling earlier when he'd put the ice to her neck. If only he hadn't glimpsed the vulnerability she hid from the world, he would have gone ahead with his plans. But as it was he couldn't.

Her questions in the car, that soft tone not at all like the Assistant District Attorney voice asking him if she'd hurt him had changed something inside him. He still wanted justice for the past. But he was coming to realize that revenge wasn't going to be enough. He wanted something…more from Sophia.

Something he was very much afraid she'd never be able to give him.

Her feet were bare and he knew her legs were as well. He wanted to go and join her. To say the hell with the plans he'd made and just concentrate on rediscovering all of the things that made Sophia special.

He'd never admit this to anyone but a part of him was very afraid that he wasn't going to be able to walk away from her this time. That he'd want to believe the promise in her eyes...that this time things might work and then when she left he'd be devastated again.

He looked around the condo. There were no memories here. No signs of the past and that should be enough to remind them—him—that there was nothing between them but a weekend of hot sex.

Hot sex. Was there any other kind with Sophia? He'd had plans of making her dress in naughty lingerie but he knew the more toys and props he used, the easier it would be for her to distance the real woman from the event. And he wanted to scratch more than the surface of her emotions. He wanted to force her out of the shell labeled Assistant District Attorney, to peel back the layers until the real woman underneath was revealed. And then...then he'd do what he'd been craving for the last ten years. Walk away.

He only hoped he could. Because when Sophia looked at him with her clear blue eyes and asked him things like had he thought he was in love with her, it made it hard for him to keep his mind focused on regaining face. It made it very hard for him to remember that there wasn't always this soft sweet woman who seemed genuinely sorry about how things had ended.

He took the rest of the things into the master bedroom suite and found the dress he'd bought for her to wear. He grabbed the slinky sandals and exited the room. Stopping at the stereo system, he put on the Stevie Ray Vaughan CD he'd brought with him. The system in the condo was state-of-the-art and there were speakers in every room. He pushed the button for the outside speakers, then crossed the room.

She glanced up as he stepped onto the porch. Her large-framed sunglasses hid her eyes and she'd donned her straw hat. She looked like a woman very accustomed to leisure.

''Nice music,'' she said as he approached. She handed him a glass of wine. He tossed the dress on the back of his chair before sitting down.

He stretched his legs out in front of him and looked out over the ocean, so different in looks and temperament from his beloved Pacific. But there was something soothing about being this close to the water.

He was acutely aware of Sophia sitting next to him and for the first time he realized that she was trying to project a relaxed attitude, but her fingers were clenched tightly in her lap. On her lips was a vague smile and she tilted her head back as if she were enjoying the music, but he sensed she wasn't.

"What are you thinking?" he asked.

"That if you had sent any other CD I would have considered our going up against each other in court a simple rivalry."

"But this CD?"

"We share the same memories."

"We do. Some of mine are so vivid. I can't hear 'Shake For Me' without thinking of you." Sophia had loved it from the first moment she'd heard it.

"Me too," she confessed softly. Placing her wineglass on the table she fingered the velvet ribbon at her throat.

"You want me to recreate it?" she asked after a few minutes.

Yes and no. He wanted new memories; he was tired of the old ones and he knew he'd be revisiting this balcony in his mind for a long, long time. "I want you to change into this dress I bought for you."

She held her hand out to him but he shook his head. "Come here."

She did and he pulled her into his lap. He lowered his head and kissed her. It felt like forever since he'd had her lips under his. Her mouth opened for his tongue and he plumbed her depths, tasting the wine and an essence that was uniquely Sophia.

She wrapped her arms around his shoulders and kissed him back. He swept his hands down her back, rubbing the line of her spine until it gave way to the curves of her buttocks. He cupped her full curves in his hands. Sophia was the most sensual woman he'd ever had in his arms and he realized he didn't want to let her go again. Yet he knew he had to.

He pulled back. Her straw hat had fallen off and her sunglasses were askew. She straddled his lap, her skirt high on her legs and her arms still around his shoulders.

"I like your lips fresh-kissed," he said, rubbing his thumb over her bottom one. She took her sunglasses off and tossed them on the table.

"What else do you like?"

"Don't you remember?"

"Every night in my dreams," she said.

"Well we don't have to dream tonight. Shake for me, babe?"

She stood up. "Here? On the balcony?"

He looked up and down the desert beach. The sun

had set and the dusk was deepening around them. The landscape lighting was two floors down and the only light that spilled from the open living room door was faint.

No witnesses to his ultimate destruction, just the moon rising ever so slowly out over the Atlantic. He leaned back in his chair and watched as Sophia moved the table and other chair out of the way. Then she went back into the house and started the song over on the CD player. He braced himself for the sight of her.

But he hadn't counted on seeing the emotion in her eyes that told him this wasn't a game to her any more.

12

SOPHIA LET THE MUSIC roll through her. She remembered Mitch in the car, teasing her and playing at a game she hoped he no longer wanted to win. She went to her overnight bag and removed the underwear she'd packed.

She pulled on the high cut lace thong and matching strapless bra with demi-cups. Over top she put on a filmy shirt and a short skirt.

She remembered his voice when he'd talked to his friend. The way he'd refused to talk about anything emotional made her realize that Mitch was still protecting himself, as he always had. Why hadn't she realized it before? Her actions in Cambridge had been motivated by her need to make him react. She sank to the rattan chair by the balcony door.

She'd forgotten how cold Mitch could be, and how he'd refused to talk about his emotions, which made her feel she was the only one who was vulnerable. The only one who was falling headlong into something she couldn't control. The only one who was emotionally vested in their relationship, and in the end he'd proved her right.

Or had he? A man who could wait ten years to come back for revenge wasn't unemotional.

"Sophia?"

She stood up and knew that she had this weekend to make some changes and some decisions. But not right now. Now she had the chance to enjoy herself with a man for the first time in a really long time.

She moved slowly toward Mitch. He was sprawled in his chair like a big lion waiting for his lioness. She heard Stevie singing *wow me baby*. And she decided to do just that. She knew what Mitch liked. What she liked.

Her hips picked up the rhythm and each step toward Mitch was seduction. He just sat there and watched her with those gray eyes that were no longer so cold. She let her skirt swish around her legs with each step she took and spun around in front of him, letting the hem fly up so that he caught a glimpse of her bare butt cheeks. She danced around his chair.

Running her finger down his arm, she took his hand in hers and slid it up and down her leg while she gyrated next to him. Then she took a step back from him and took the hem of her shirt in her hands. She rubbed the material against her skin, loving the sensation of silk on her body. She pulled it up, slowly revealing her midriff and abdomen, then she lifted it higher so that the lower edge of her bra was visible.

"Want to see more?" she asked, pitching her voice low.

"What do you think?"

She winked at him. "If you're still thinking I've got to work harder."

She pulled the shirt over her head and tossed it to him. He caught the silk and held it briefly to his face before setting it on the floor next to him. She danced toward him again, scarcely aware of anything other than Mitch.

She shimmied toward him, hips moving with exaggerated slowness and as she got closer she fumbled with the zipper in the back of her skirt, then released it, but not all the way, just enough so that it slid low on her hips, revealing her belly button and the top of her panties.

She shook her hips back and forth to let the fabric and gravity slowly reveal the rest of her body. She followed the path of the material with her hands. Then slowly, she skimmed her own hands up her torso, cupping her breasts through her lacy bra. She felt the waistband of her skirt fall past her hips and linger on her thighs. She spread her legs to hold the material there, and teased him with her clothing half off for a few beats before she let the skirt fall to her feet.

She stepped over the small puddle of silk and moved closer to Mitch. She skimmed her gaze over him. His erection strained the crotch of his pants. She danced into his range and he reached for her but she took a step back.

Her bra had a front clasp and she unfastened it but kept the cups over her breasts, peeling one back slowly and watching his eyes narrow as her hard nipple was revealed to him. She covered the aroused flesh back up and then showed him the other before pivoting on her heel and strutting a few paces away from him.

She dipped at the waist and glanced at him between her spread legs. His hands were rubbing along his thighs and she mimicked the action with her hands on the back of her legs. She dropped her bra to the floor. She straightened and paced back to him stopping in front of his chair breathing hard. She lifted her leg, bracing her foot between his spread thighs, and leaned forward over him so the tip of one breast dangled right in front of his mouth.

His breath brushed over her nipple each time he exhaled. Warm and moist she shivered in anticipation, leaning closer to him so that he'd take the hint and suckle her.

But Mitch reached behind him for the dress he'd carried onto the balcony earlier.

"Put this on," he said, his voice a husky rasp.

"You don't really want me to get dressed," she said.

He put his hands on her waist and lifted her away from him. "Yes, I do."

He stood and walked out of the apartment. Sophia could only stand there clutching the dress. She realized then however her feelings had changed, Mitch's hadn't, and nothing short of complete and utter devastation of her emotions was going to satisfy him.

MITCH WALKED long and hard, striding away from the condo and Sophia. He'd left to prove something to himself that he was still in control. God, that was a joke. Now as he paced down the nearly empty beach he acknowledged to himself that Sophia was his downfall.

He sought to find his control. God, he was known as the ice man in and out of court. What a joke that was. He wasn't anywhere near ice-cold when Sophia was in the vicinity.

His cell phone rang and he thought about not answering it. He had his own problems to sort out but only two people would call on this number. One was Sophia and the other was Dev. He didn't want to talk to either of them. He unclipped the phone from his belt and glanced at the caller ID screen. Dev.

"What's up, Dev?"

"I'm...oh, God man. I'm sitting outside her house and I don't think I'm going to be able to do it."

"Julie's?"

"Yes. What would you do?"

Mitch thought about confessing his weaknesses to Sophia—he didn't think he'd be able to do it. Something in his makeup demanded he be the strong one. He realized that only as Dev waited on the other end of the line.

"I'm not the right one to ask."

"Why not? You're the golden boy. The successful one of the two of us."

"I wish."

"What are you saying?"

"That if it were me I'd cut my losses and move on. You're braver than me, Dev. You let the whole world see your weaknesses."

"Not the whole world, only you," Dev said.

Mitch thought about all of his relationships and he was honest enough to admit he didn't have that many. He'd used what had happened with Sophia as the reason he never let anyone close. But here was his oldest friend and Mitch knew he always kept

Dev at arm's length as well, always let Dev be the vulnerable one. "I can't do that."

"Sure you can. What's your weakness?" Dev asked after a few minutes of silence passed. He knew his friend was delaying the moment when he had to go in and talk to Julie. He knew that Dev would go in there. In some ways Dev was better at relationships than Mitch was.

"Sophia."

"The college babe?"

So funny to hear someone else talking about Sophia. "Yeah, her."

"Revenge not sweet?"

It was sweet but by the same token it was bitter and hard to swallow, and he didn't know what he wanted any more. That wasn't like him. He set goals and achieved them, and then moved on. It was why he'd become one of the most successful lawyers in L.A. "What are you going to do, Dev?"

"I don't know."

"What a pair we are."

"Dammit. I'm going in there." Mitch heard the warning buzzer as Dev opened his car door, then heard him walking up some sort of gravel sidewalk.

"Go for it."

"You should too. If revenge doesn't work, then let it go."

"At what price?"

"I've got to be honest man, I'm miserable as it is, it can't get worse."

Dev hung up and Mitch thought about what his friend had said. Weaknesses were a funny thing. Mitch studied his ones in court and spent a lot of time trying to turn them into strengths. Maybe he should do the same with Sophia. Make her his strength.

But a part of him didn't trust her and he wasn't sure he ever would.

He walked back to the condo and let himself back in. The scent of garlic and oregano greeted him and he carefully climbed the stairs, unsure what mood Sophia would be in when he returned.

He found her in the kitchen listening to Stevie Ray Vaughan still and stirring something in a sizzling frying pan. She swayed slowly to the music and he wondered for a moment if anything he did affected her as deeply as she did him. This woman didn't appear to have any weaknesses and that made him feel like he was standing in the cold again.

He cleared his throat. She faced him and he saw in her eyes the lingering pain. She crossed her arms over her chest and leaned back against the countertop. Bastard, Mitch thought. If any other man had done to Sophia what he'd just done, Mitch would have kicked his ass.

"We need to talk," he said.

She turned off the burner and moved to the middle of the room, keeping the table between them. "Yes, we do. We need to set up a few rules."

"For?"

"This weekend. I don't mind being your slave but I don't want to be tortured. If you're going to arouse us both and walk away again, I'm not staying."

"I'm sorry. That wasn't fair to you."

"Why'd you do it?" she asked.

He moved closer to her, then stopped at the opposite side of the table and watched her carefully. "To prove to myself I could."

She said nothing for long minutes and then reached behind her back to untie the apron she had on. She folded it carefully and put it in the center of the table. "Then I'll call a cab."

Well, he'd done it. He'd hurt her and forced her to leave him. Alone again. But he wasn't ready for the end. Not yet. He grabbed her wrist to stop her.

She half turned toward him.

"Don't. Sophia. Don't go."

SOPHIA STOOD STILL and watched the man who'd been the greatest influence over her. She was still aching for his possession. Cursing her own frailty where he was concerned, she tried to remind herself that she deserved better.

She knew leaving him was what she should do.

But tonight in this homey little kitchen with its cheery yellow walls leaving wasn't something she wanted to do.

If she stayed, she wanted this weekend to be a time of healing, to mend whatever lingering resentment the both of them had from the past. And she knew she had her fair share of it.

"Why do you want me to stay?" she asked. Her control was a distant memory and she knew that she wasn't leaving. No matter what she might say to Mitch, she wasn't walking out of this condo until she'd had at least one night with her former lover. There was too much between them for her to simply walk away.

"Don't make me say it."

She stood there, not sure this was going to work. She should escape while she still could, and write this whole episode off as a bad debt. But she didn't want to leave Mitch.

Was Mitch as deeply affected by her as she was by him? Why hadn't she realized before that something this strong had to cut both ways? Now she had to figure out if they were the same sides of the coin or if they were the opposites—one acting out of affection, the other out of spite.

Knowing she'd always protected herself, hidden a part of herself from Mitch, she decided that this time she wouldn't. She couldn't expect him to deal honestly with her if she didn't do the same. She was taking a bigger risk with Mitch than she'd ever taken before. She was gambling with something that she knew was more important than her career, even if she'd never admit to it out loud. "I've shown you more of myself than I have any other man."

"Really?" he asked.

He wasn't going to let her throw out statements and pretend they passed for genuine emotion. He was going to make her do a different kind of strip-tease, the kind where you revealed your soul. "Yes. I hate that you know me best. But there it is. Kind of sad when you think about it."

"No, it's not. I think you might be the only person I've ever let glimpse parts of me."

"Why?" she asked, inviting him to bare a little bit of his soul so that she wouldn't feel so very vulnerable.

"I've never been able to figure it out. But I know that I need you here with me this weekend."

He dropped her hand and reached for her neck, unfastening the black velvet ribbon and dropping it on the table. "Stay if you want to. But stay as my equal, not my slave."

"I...I want to talk, Mitch. I want to learn all about you this time."

He said nothing, only stared at her. She began to

feel acutely embarrassed and wondered if she'd asked him for too much.

"I'd stay for sex," she said, wanting him to understand that he didn't have to give her what she'd asked for. If he wanted her for the weekend, and then never again, she wouldn't hold it against him.

"It's more than sex. But that's a big part of it."

"Sex always was. I was a little ashamed today in the car that I'd never asked about your family."

"I never asked about yours."

"Why didn't we do that?"

"I'm not sure I care," he said.

Too much honesty wasn't a good thing, she realized. She felt awkward and shy. She'd set the table for dinner not sure what to expect when Mitch returned.

The table looked ordinary. Any couple staying together would set it the same way. It gave a legitimacy to this weekend that she wondered if it ever really would have.

"Let's eat dinner first."

"You cook?"

"There's a lot about me you don't know, Mitch."

"Let's use this weekend to rectify that. Why'd you make the wager with me?"

"I wanted some closure. I didn't like the way things ended between us any more than you did."

"At least you got a job out of it," he said.

"Yes, I got the job but nothing was the same after you left."

"For me, either," he confessed. Something changed in Mitch's stance, something that made her feel special.

"I made chicken for dinner," she said at long last. She knew she was using food as a barrier.

"I'm not really hungry for chicken," he said, tugging her closer to him.

She snuggled into his arms, resting her head on his shoulder. "What do you want? There's some veggies and I could make a Greek salad."

"Salad won't satisfy me either."

"Mitch?"

"Enough talking. I want to take you to bed and make love to you."

She shivered at the words. She wanted the same thing. She had wanted it since she'd walked into her office and saw that tub of Coronas on her desk. He bent and lifted her in his arms and carried her down the hallway to the master bedroom. Lowering his head, he took her mouth in a kiss that promised the beginning of something that Sophia was afraid to believe in.

13

Mitch took Sophia's mouth with his. She tasted of wine and tears, and though he hadn't seen her cry he knew he'd hurt her. God, he had known that before he'd kissed her.

He'd had enough of talking. He wanted to make her his, and make up for the pain they'd both caused each other.

In three strides he was at the bed. He set Sophia on her feet and peeled back the covers. He toed off his loafers and reached down to remove his socks. She was barefoot and wore only the dress he'd purchased for her. She looked exquisite in it. It was short and filmy, plunging between her breasts and revealing the creamy white tops of each one, and ending high on her thigh.

He cupped her breasts, pushing them together. Her cleavage swelled above the bodice of her dress.

He lowered his head and traced the edge where fabric met skin with his tongue. She smelled of perfume and a natural womanly scent that he associated only with Sophia. He closed his eyes and buried his face between her breasts, inhaling deeply.

Shifting slightly to the right, he tasted her again with languid strokes of his tongue. Her skin was sweeter and more addicting than anything he'd ever tasted before. He followed the curve of her breast from top to bottom, the texture changing as he reached the edge of her nipple.

The velvety nub beckoned him and he pushed the fabric of her dress out of the way. He wanted to see her.

"Stand here."

He crossed the room and flipped on the light switch, flooding the room with light. Sophia stood where he had left her, her dark hair hanging around her shoulders in long curls. Her lips were full and lush, wet and swollen from his kisses. Her breast spilt from the fabric, full and white, topped with hard little berries that made his mouth water.

He crossed back to her side in less than two strides. "That's better."

"Is it?" she asked.

"I want to see you, Sophia. The real you, not the dream that's been haunting me."

He didn't give her a chance to respond. He might once again be playing the fool but right now he didn't care.

He lowered his head once more to the full globe

of her left breast, scraping the aroused nipple with his teeth. She shuddered in his arms. He used his hand to stimulate her other nipple. He circled it with his finger and ran his nail across the center very carefully while at the same time using his teeth on the first one.

She moaned his name, undulating against him. Her hands swept down his body and she unzipped his pants. His cock sprang into her waiting hands. He wanted her to grasp the length of him but instead she only teased him by running her finger up and down the sides of his shaft.

He suckled her nipple and slid one hand down her body. Up under her skirt, he encountered the sexy thong he'd seen on her earlier. As he caressed her sticky curls through the lace, she reached between his legs to cup his balls and play with them gently. She scraped the edge of her fingernail up his cock and then took him in her hand and pulled upward with just the right strength.

He couldn't wait much longer. He slipped his touch inside the crotch of her panties and pushed two fingers into her humid opening. She moaned and lifted her leg to give him deeper access.

He shifted and they almost toppled over. He turned and fell backward on the bed. Sophia braced her hands on his chest and leaned up over him. Their groins pressed together. She bit her lower lip and rotated on him. Spreading her cream down his length. It felt deliciously hot and he wanted nothing more than to let her rock against him until they both came. Later, he thought.

He pulled her down to him and rolled until she was underneath him again. "Gotta be on top?" she asked.

"It's a male thing."

"Why?"

"I did win," he reminded her.

He didn't want to say any more but for once he wanted to feel as though he was really in control. Control of their lovemaking and in control of this woman who gave away so little.

He tore his shirt off and tossed it across the room and then kicked his pants down. He reached for the bodice of Sophia's dress and tugged until the fabric ripped, leaving her body bare.

He slid his hand down to her panties.

"Stop."

He did, glancing up at her. She reached underneath her body and pushed the panties down her legs. "I like these."

He chuckled. "Me too."

He bent his head and followed the path of her skimpy underwear with his mouth. Some of her wetness had rubbed against her thigh and he licked her clean. Then he rose over her.

He bent her legs back against her body, leaving her totally exposed to him. Leaning down, he tasted her very pink flesh. Caressing her carefully with his tongue until her hips were rising against him and her hands clenched in his hair. He slid up her body, holding her hips in his hands, tilting them upward to give him greater access.

He grabbed one of the pillows from the head of the bed and wedged it under her, then, draping her thighs over his arms, he brought their bodies together. Sophia reached between them and grasped his dick, guiding it to her entrance.

"Take me," she said.

He did. He entered her deeply and completely, stopping only when he was fully within her. He felt her clench around him. Knowing she was doing it intentionally. He smiled at her. He lowered his head and took her mouth, mimicking the movements of his hips with his tongue and soon he felt close to the edge. It wasn't going to be much longer until he climaxed.

She rotated her hips against him with each thrust and soon she was gasping for breath and making those sweet sounds of pre-orgasm. He reared back, so he could go deeper, her feet on his shoulders.

He held her still for his thrusts and she tilted her head back, her eyes closing as her orgasm rushed over her. He felt the tingling at the base of his spine and then emptied himself into her. Her legs slipped down to his side and he fell on the bed next to her on his back.

SOPHIA DIDN'T WANT to think. For once in her life she wasn't going to analyze the consequences of her actions, then plot out her next move. Earlier alone in the kitchen she'd realized there was no way to come out a winner and she'd decided to cut her losses.

She struggled to calm her racing breath. Thoroughly exhausted, she lay on her back with her hand over her eyes and pretended nothing had changed.

Pretended that walking away or watching Mitch walk away after this weekend wouldn't affect her. She still had her career. She still had the promise of the job she'd worked long and hard for. Pretended that she hadn't rediscovered her worst fear.

Mitch reached over and pulled her against his side. She nestled into his arms. He rubbed his hand up and down her back bringing tingling nerve endings to attention once again.

But the kiss he dropped on the top of her head was infinitely sweet and not meant to arouse. Mitch had never been a talker after sex. He'd kind of been the roll over and go to sleep kind of guy. And she hoped he still was.

She needed a moment to get her defenses back in

order. She didn't want him to know or see how deeply their lovemaking had affected her. Why had she ever thought this would be different this time? The last time when she'd been a young woman she'd nearly lost herself in the incredible feelings he'd elicited. But this time, she was a self-assured person. She knew who she was and what she liked. Or did she?

She sensed Mitch watching her and closed her eyes quickly, feigning sleep. Coward, her inner voice taunted her. When had she forgotten her golden rule—never back down.

She opened her eyes and pushed herself up so that she rested on her elbow and stared down at Mitch.

She heard a rumble from his stomach and then his embarrassed laugh.

"Hungry?" she asked, tiptoeing her fingers down his chest. He inhaled sharply and caught her fingers just above his belly button. He rubbed her hand over his chest before bringing it to his lips and dropping a very soft kiss in the center.

"Yeah, I guess I'm obvious."

If only. He was a big mystery to her and always had been. She felt she had to struggle not to broadcast everything she felt for him. "I can finish making dinner."

"Sounds good," he said, tugging her down into his arms again.

He continued to hold her, stroking her back and pressing his face against her neck. She was happy to lie in his arms for those long minutes and shut out the rest of the world.

Except she knew she couldn't keep the world at bay and she'd intended this weekend to be a time of healing. Realizing then that she'd feel pain on Monday morning regardless of how the weekend had played out, she decided to drop the barrier she used to protect herself a little.

She turned her head and brushed her lips against his pectoral and the muscle jumped under her lips. She smiled against his flesh and the rubbing motion of his hands changed. No longer soothing languid strokes but deliberate touches against the sides of her breast.

His stomach rumbled again.

"Well, I know where your mind is," she said.

"I swear that's not where my mind is," he said with a devilish grin.

"Come on, lover boy. I don't want you passing out on me." She got up from the bed and picked up her dress. Clearly she wouldn't be wearing it again.

"I'm not going to apologize."

"I'm not going to ask you to."

He snagged his pants from the floor. She grabbed his shirt but he stopped her. "I've got something for you."

Going to his suitcase, he rummaged around in it for a minute, tossing her a very colorful silk scarf. The scarf was large enough to be worn. She held the fabric in her hands, running her fingers down the length of it.

Mitch came back to her side and ran his hand down the side of her arm, taking the fabric from her. "I'll help you."

His voice was husky, his eyes dilated and his nostrils flared. She nodded her acquiescence.

He opened the scarf and draped it around behind her. Using the material to draw her forward, he pulled her closer until their chests touched, then lowered his mouth to hers. His kiss was infinitely sweet and shocking. He didn't touch her anywhere except for the brush of his chest with each breath he took and the gentle touch of his lips on hers.

But she felt surrounded by him. She felt lost in his arms and this time it was more than lust that made her insides clench. It was a longing for something she'd denied she'd wanted for a long time. Something tender and real—something she'd never realized that Mitch had to give to her until this moment.

And that something was magic. The magical ability to call from her soul, dreams she'd forgotten long ago. Promises she'd made a lifetime earlier before she'd left her parents' home to go to college. Before she'd started her very prominent career. Before she'd made a wager with the only man who'd ever made her feel fulfilled.

SOPHIA'S RESPONSES HAD always been addictive, and tonight was no different. She surrendered herself to the moment in a way he'd never be able to. For being one of the most composed and driven people he'd ever met, she was also one of the most sensual.

She had her eyes closed and her head tipped back to grant him easier access to her mouth.

Sophia felt incredible in his arms and it was all he could do not to forget his empty stomach and take her back to bed. But if he'd learned anything about himself it was that he had to control his desires for those things that he wanted the most.

He wasn't going to let Sophia be his Achilles' heel again, but she tasted so good, felt so right in his arms that he didn't want to let her go. He closed his eyes, savoring Sophia in his arms.

His stomach growled again and he cursed under his breath. She laughed but it was more of a nervous giggle. "Are we taking too long to get to the kitchen?"

He shrugged. Bringing the ends of the scarf together, he wrapped them around her neck and tied it in the back. The colorful material now made a halter-style dress. She was covered but the knowledge that she was bare underneath and he only had to untie one knot to get to her aroused another hunger.

She led the way back to the kitchen. It felt like a lifetime since he'd returned and found her at the stove. She picked up the apron and tied it around her waist.

He watched her move toward the stove and turn on the burner. The real Sophia blended with his long-ago fantasy of her. He knew this was his secret dream, the one he'd never shared with anyone.

This tiny kitchen in the condo disappeared and he saw her standing in the huge kitchen in his home in California. Saw a bottle of open Chardonnay on the counter and heard the sounds of their children playing in the background.

It was his secret fantasy and for a moment he was tempted like Adam to believe he could live in Eden and have it all. But Mitch was a modern man and he knew no one had it all. Least of all him.

Sophia was staring at him. He realized she must have asked him something but had no idea what.

"Mitch, you okay?"

"Yeah. Did you need me to do something for you?" he asked. He fiddled with the dial on the kitchen radio until a jazz station came on.

"No. I asked you to tell me about your friend—the one who called on the way here."

"Dev?"

"Is that his name?"

"Yes. Why do you want to know about him?"

"I want to understand you."

He stiffened. The idea of revealing himself was an altogether scary prospect. "I don't know what you mean."

"I want to know more."

Sophia was the only woman to hurt him in ways he'd never understood he could be hurt. He knew he didn't want to show her any more of his vulnerabilities, and Dev was definitely a weak point.

"What are you going to tell me?" he asked.

She tilted her head to the side, a sparkle in her eyes. Wearing only a scarf, with her hair hanging around her shoulders, she wasn't exactly intimidating. "You want to negotiate?"

"Yes, counselor, I do."

She put down her wooden spatula and crossed her arms. "I'll tell you…what do you want to know about me?"

"I want to know about your family. You never talked about them."

"Deal," she said, turning back to the stove and adding chicken from the fridge into the frying pan.

"You first," she said, while Steely Dan's "Babylon Sister" played from the radio. Her hips swayed to the music as she sauntered back to the stove.

Mitch took out two Coronas and sliced up a lime. He handed one to Sophia and leaning back against the counter watched her for a minute.

"Anytime now," she said.

He knew he wouldn't be able to stall for long. A month ago he'd have known what to say about Dev. But everything had changed between them, and Mitch had come to realize that Dev and he weren't really all that different, it was only how they dealt with their problems that was different. "I'm trying to decide where to start. I've known Dev my entire life."

"I didn't have any friendships that lasted from elementary school or for that matter any school."

"Our folks were friends and we grew up in the same neighborhood.

"So familiarity is responsible for your friendship?"

"Nah," he said, taking another drag on the Corona. He played idly with a wedge of lime that was lying on the counter.

"Dev and I are like two halves of the same coin."

"Where did he go to college?"

Mitch didn't want to talk about Dev any more. He picked up the lime and set his beer bottle on the table. He moved slowly around behind Sophia, leaning over her to see what she was doing.

"What are you doing?"

"Seeing if lime tastes as good as I remember."

"I thought you were hungry."

"You keep cooking."

"Yes, sir."

He untied the knot behind her neck, and tucked the ends under her arms so that the scarf stayed in place. He swept her hair up with one hand and lowered his mouth, tasting her.

She shivered and he smiled against her skin. He reached for the lime, squeezed a couple of drops on the back of her neck, and then laved them with his tongue.

"Taste the same?"

"Mmm-hmm, delicious."

Mitch slipped his arms around Sophia and held her as she finished fixing their dinner. She didn't say anything and neither did he but he knew that something primal in him had shifted and changed.

14

THEY ATE QUICKLY and cleaned up the kitchen as if they'd done it together a million times. Sophia realized how much of herself she'd hidden from Mitch during college, and how much of herself she'd denied in the intervening years.

It was a sobering moment, a moment that made her realize that she'd never really risked herself, which had made it easier for her to choose her career back then.

The Deputy D.A. position weighed on the back of her mind. She realized now why Joan had wanted to wait to hear her answer. Not that Sophia wasn't going to take the job, it just gave her a moment's pause to realize there were other parts of herself she had yet to realize.

She liked to cook. She liked domesticity but she submerged those things because they didn't further her career goals. But tonight when she'd stood at the stove cooking she realized that it was soothing in some way to putter and listen to the radio.

"Let's go for a walk," Mitch said.

"Let me change," she said.

"You're decent. Let's go."

But she didn't feel decent. As soon as she'd swallowed the last bite of her dinner, he'd pulled her around the table onto his lap. He'd freed his erection and thrust into her. It had been incredible.

She smelled like sex now and anyone they encountered on the beach would know what they'd done. But there was a sparkle in Mitch's eyes that she was reluctant to dismiss. He hadn't ever seemed this young, this carefree and she wanted to keep him in this mood.

For once she was enjoying herself and not worrying about a future that would come regardless of her plans. For once she was just Sophia and she'd forgotten how liberating that was.

"Okay."

She took his hand in hers as they walked down the stairs toward the beach. The moon was full and the beach nearly deserted. The sand under her feet was cool.

"I believe you still have to tell me about your family."

"What do you want to know about them?" she asked. She rarely talked about her family. She was a disappointment to her family. Not married and no prospects of ever being married. Being Italian she was supposed to have provided ample offspring by this time.

"My parents live in Arizona. They retired there a few years ago. But they spend most of their time in New Jersey visiting my grandparents and going to Atlantic City."

"So gambling is a family trait?" he asked, arching one eyebrow at her in a way she found endearing.

"Ha. I never gamble."

"Must be my bad influence."

"Must be. What about your parents?"

"They live in California. About twenty minutes from me. I have dinner with them every Sunday. My older brother and his family come too."

Her heart gave a funny little lurch at his words. She'd never pictured Mitch at home. Never imagined what his family would be like but they sounded lovely. Like her own family, who she loved very much, even though they tried to nag her into marrying and having kids. No matter how disappointed they were in her, they still loved her.

"What about you? Any siblings?"

"Yes, two brothers. Both older and both very Italian."

"What's that mean?"

She struggled to find the words to describe her brothers. They were like younger versions of her dad. "Exactly what you think it might mean. They are…macho, I guess. I don't know how their wives put up with them. I mean I love them, but they're bossy and they know it all."

Mitch laughed. "You could be describing yourself."

"I'm macho?" she asked.

He tugged her closer to him, and the warmth of his body surrounded her. "You're deliberately misunderstanding me."

"Am I, counselor? Perhaps you should've pondered your question a bit before asking it."

"Sophia," he said her name like more of a growl than a word.

She wrinkled her nose. She loved sparring with him. It had been fun in front of the judge, but she'd been too preoccupied with trying to win their bet to be able to enjoy it. Here though on the beach with Mitch so near her, she could enjoy playing word games with him. "I had expected more from an attorney of your reputation."

He lifted her up and carried her into the surf, holding her suspended over the waves. She knew he wouldn't drop her. It was too shallow here. But she felt the spray from the curl of each wave.

"Intimidation? I'd expected better of you."

"Evasion? I expected better of you."

She looked into his eyes, wrapping her arms around his shoulders. "I like surprising you."

He lowered his head and kissed her. It was deep and carnal and reminded her that he was real, and that this wasn't one of the many dreams that had tormented her. Mitch was here in the moon-drenched night. Why were they talking about families?

"You always do," he said against her lips.

"Really?"

"Yes."

There was a certain pressure that went with knowing he had some expectations from her. She knew he'd meant the words in a nice way. Still she couldn't help but remember the last time she'd surprised him.

She'd betrayed him long ago in Cambridge. She only hoped this time she could trust herself and her heart enough to stay with Mitch.

MITCH CARRIED Sophia out of the surf and sank to the ground. He maneuvered their bodies until Sophia was sitting between his legs, resting her back against his chest. He forced himself to hold her loosely. He knew he couldn't keep her if she didn't want to stay with him.

He wanted to know more about her, to understand what made her tick. Learning about her brothers gave him a key to her. She'd had to fight against what they wanted her to be, and he wondered if she hadn't felt the same way with him.

"You never mentioned your mom. What's she like?" he asked. It would be easy to make love to her now on the beach and leave the conversation behind. That's what his gut told him to do. But if he'd learned anything it was that Sophia wasn't just an itch to be scratched. She'd become embedded in his soul and he didn't think he'd ever be free of her.

Sophia tipped her head back, looking up at the stars. He watched her profile. The angles of her nose and chin. The long elegant length of her neck. He lifted his hand and touched her softly.

She closed her eyes and sighed as he caressed the line of her neck.

"Tell me about your mom," he said again.

"She's brilliant. She's so smart and sharp…" Her voice trailed off and he suspected she was seeing something in her head. A vision of her mom. He wondered if Mrs. Deltonio looked like Sophia. He'd like to meet her and talk to her and find out the secret dreams of Sophia that she guarded so carefully.

"Very like her daughter," he said. "Is she a lawyer?"

Sophia turned to face him, her eyes very serious and guarded. He realized he'd stumbled onto something he'd never expected to find. This area of Sophia's life was highly personal.

"Are you kidding? She's a housewife."

He knew that in Sophia's words was the truth he'd been searching for since he'd come back into her life. The motivation she had for every action she'd taken, but for the life of him he couldn't figure it out.

His mom had been a stay-at-home mom but she also kept the books for his dad's hardware store. His parents had valued the partnership they had. Combining work and home had completed them in a way that Mitch wanted for himself.

"Is that why you haven't settled down?" he asked. Did she fear turning into her mom?

"Kind of. She could've been anything but instead her dad told her to marry my dad and my mom gave up her career to raise kids and tend to my father's every need."

"Is she bitter?" he asked. His sister-in-law Corrine loved staying home with her kids. Which had surprised everyone in the family including Corrine, who used to work in publicity for one of the big studios. In a quiet moment last summer she'd told Mitch that she realized she'd been filling her life with lots of unimportant things until she had her kids and husband.

"No. I asked her about it one time. And she said she loved taking care of the family."

"And you knew you never could be?" he asked without thinking.

"Is that what you believe?"

He shrugged. Why the hell had he started this conversation? He should reach out and untie the knot holding her scarf in place and then lead her into the ocean and make love to her.

"I'm waiting," she said in a very lawyerly tone that told him there was no getting out of this.

"You don't have a steady guy in your life," he pointed out.

"You're right, I don't. But then the men I meet are usually in my profession and don't see me as anything other than a D.A."

"Why not?"

"I wonder sometimes if it isn't me."

He had no answer to that. Sophia projected an image that said she could take care of herself. A man had to watch his balls around her and that could be either very dangerous or exciting.

"That's part of your appeal," he said.

"What is?"

"That challenge of your attitude. It says I can take care of myself without a man, so why should I take a chance."

"I hadn't realized that was how I appeared."

"Am I wrong?" he asked.

"Yes, you are."

"Who was the last important man in your life?"

"Honestly?"

"Of course."

She took a deep breath. "You."

"Me?"

"Yes."

"Then why'd you leave me like that?" he asked. He suspected it stemmed from the fear of losing herself. He hadn't understood it then, but now it made a bit more sense.

"I don't know."

"I find that hard to believe. I thought I made you doubt who you were." Weren't those the words she'd used to justify her actions from long ago?

"When you say it, I sound like a flake. But it ties back to my mom. I've always been afraid that I would like having a family and taking care of my husband too much. That's the real reason why I jumped at that intern spot all those years ago.

"I knew if it came down to it, choosing between you and a career that I'd be tempted to choose you. And I didn't have any idea how you'd react to that."

He said nothing. She couldn't have known that he'd intended her to be his bride. He had dreams of them working together for the big firm for a few years, then once they'd learned enough, maybe returning to the West Coast and starting their own small firm.

"Still like my surprises?" she asked.

He realized he'd been silent too long, but he didn't really know how to respond to that. She'd just told him that if he hadn't been afraid to let her see his vulnerabilities, they could have had a life together that would have exceeded both of their expectations. Holding her in his arms and knowing that, he still couldn't say the words that would let her know how much he needed her.

He untied the knot at the back of her neck and brushed the scarf down off her body. He knew he was evading her question but didn't care. He couldn't talk any more tonight. He didn't even want to think. He wanted just to feel Sophia.

He stood and pushed off his pants. "Let's go for a swim."

She took his hand and they walked into the water together. What she'd revealed had brought all those emotions he'd denied having for her to the surface.

KNOWING SHE'D SAID TOO MUCH, Sophia didn't wait for Mitch to make the first move. As soon as they were waist-deep in the water, she dove in and swam away from him. They were in a secluded little cove area where the waves small, and the water shallow so they could swim comfortably.

"Now I'll show you evasion."

"I'm not sure you can win at this game," he said, diving in after her.

She waited until he surfaced. "Catch me if you can."

"You're on."

He grabbed for her, but she dove into a wave and when she surfaced she didn't see him. Under the water she felt something brush the inside of her left thigh. She dove and kicked a little farther out to sea.

Again when she surfaced she didn't see Mitch, but this time she felt his fingers caressing the crease in her buttocks. She shivered with awareness.

Reaching out blindly under the water she found his erection and encircled it with her hand, tugging on it once and then quickly kicking away.

She surfaced again and didn't see him. Suddenly he came up behind her in the surf, his arms curling around to grasp her breasts. He nipped at the shell of her ear. "Gotcha."

She shivered. He plucked at her aroused nipples. His mouth continued to play at her neck. Sensation spread throughout her body. His erection nestled between her buttocks and she shifted a little, rubbing him between them.

One of his hands slipped down her body. He lingered at her belly button, and then slid lower, parting her nether lips. He didn't touch her, just held her open so that the seawater stimulated her clitoris. She moaned.

"Please," she gasped.

His erection was back against her buttocks again. He suckled against her neck. His hand on her breast alternated between pinching her hardened nipples and rubbing them with his palm.

She felt like a prisoner to her desire and to this man. She scissor-kicked her legs, trying to escape from Mitch's grip, but couldn't.

He chuckled in her ear. "You're mine."

Those words sounded right deep in her soul. She ignored that feeling and focused instead on the physical. She reached behind her and slipped her hand down to his cock, taking him in her grip. But he pulled his hips back, not allowing her to touch him.

"Mitch," she said.

"What, babe?" he asked. He let the motion of the waves rock his body against hers. His cock slipped from between her ass and the water felt cool by comparison.

"I..." She couldn't think, couldn't speak. She just wanted him inside her. Now.

"You can say it. You need me."

"I do."

"Say please," he said. He rubbed the fleshy part of her labia with long strokes of his fingers. First one side and then the other. She ached for his touch on her clitoris. She shifted again, trying to bring his hand where she wanted it.

But he wouldn't be budged. She shoved her own hand down her body, but he caught her before she could bring relief to herself. "Impatient?"

"You have no idea," she muttered.

He chuckled. Finally he touched her clit, just a light brush of his fingertip. She reached behind her again but he canted his hips away from her touch. "Mitch. No more games."

"Float on your back."

She did. He pushed them closer to shore when he could stand easily. He parted her legs and moved between them. "Part yourself for me. Show me where you want my tongue."

She did as he asked and felt his breath on her. She knew he was seeing her swollen with need and hungry for his mouth. He lowered his head and exhaled against her very sensitive flesh.

Her thighs twitched and she wanted to clamp her legs around his head until he brought her off. She felt his tongue against her lapping at her with increasing strength. Then she felt the edge of his teeth just scraping along the edge of her clit and she screamed.

He thrust two fingers inside her, rocking up against her G-spot while his mouth worked its magic on her. He feathered light touches alternating with rougher ones and brought her quickly to the edge of orgasm. Still she fought it off, not wanting to go over too quickly.

He added a third finger inside her body and stretched them out when he pulled back and then thrust back into her body. Everything inside her tightened and her climax rushed through her.

Mitch grabbed her by the waist, pulling her down his body until she was impaled on his length.

But he stopped there. She opened her eyes and met his gaze. "What are you waiting for?"

"You."

She shifted on him. Holding his shoulders she lifted herself off of his dick and then slowly slid back down. "Faster," he said.

"Not yet," she said.

She tightened her vagina around him, milking him as she pushed herself up his length and letting him slip out of her body.

He grabbed her hips and pulled her down while he thrust upward. He worked them together until she felt every nerve ending tingling again and her second orgasm rushed over her just as Mitch bit her neck and groaned with his own release.

15

———

MITCH DEPOSITED Sophia back at her town house on Sunday evening just as the sun was setting. The weekend, though not what he'd originally intended, had been very satisfying. The thought of leaving now, of returning to his lonely hotel room near the airport made his feet heavy.

"Want a drink before you leave?" she asked.

They were standing on her front stoop. Two teen-aged boys were skateboarding on the street. Mitch wanted to push her back in her foyer and take her one last time up against the wall. *One last time.* Damn. He wasn't ready for it to be the last time.

Sophia too seemed reluctant for their time to end. Mitch almost said yes but prolonging the inevitable wasn't a good idea.

"I better not."

She stepped away from him into the open door-way of her town house. He stayed where he was though the temptation was strong to say the hell with being sensible. Hell, when had he become so dull?

But his weary soul said dull was safer around Sophia.

"Need a good night's sleep to sit on the plane for five hours tomorrow?"

He doubted he'd sleep at all. He could still smell her every time he breathed in. He could still feel her under his hands and around his cock. He could still taste her on his tongue. "If I go inside, I know I won't want to leave."

"Mitch…" There was sadness in her voice and his heart ached a little. He wished things were different. He wished she'd never sent him on a false trail in Cambridge and left him looking like a fool. Because then he'd be able to believe that she wanted him to stay. He would be able to believe that this time she might be willing to give up her career for him, and able to believe that happy endings might still be in the stars for them.

"Don't say anything else. I'll be tempted to believe you," he said at last.

"And I'm not trustworthy?" she asked.

He took a step toward her and she recoiled. He should know by now that Sophia could be hurt in ways he'd never imagined. But old habits were hard to break.

"Babe, we've got even more working against us now than we did when we were at Harvard."

He'd tried to find a workable solution. In the wee

hours of the night when Sophia had cuddled so trustingly in his arms, he'd held her with desperation and tried to figure a way to merge their lives. There wasn't one. She was entrenched in Orlando.

And he wasn't willing to give up his life in California for her. He had that house, that big damned empty house that he'd been waiting to fill with a family since he'd returned to Los Angeles ten years ago.

"You're right. They offered me the Deputy District Attorney job before I left. So leaving now would mean sacrificing all I've worked for."

And she'd never do that. Sophia's sacrifices had started long before he met her. Over the weekend they'd talked and he'd realized how little he'd known about her. She'd put her studies first so she could get out from under her father's controlling influence and prove herself in a world that was still for the most part a man's world.

"Congratulations," he said. "You'll do well in that position."

"Thanks." She was oddly quiet. Her arms were wrapped around her waist. She wore a white silk tank top with that scarf he'd given her the first night wrapped around her waist. She had that black velvet ribbon back around her neck. Her feet were shod in simple white sandals. She looked exotic and sexy standing in front of him. Or she had when they left Boca; now she just looked…lonely.

His hungry soul clamored for him to say the hell with pretending leaving was easy and pull her into his arms. But he knew better. Sophia wasn't like other women. That was a big part of what drew him to her. That was also the number one reason why he was afraid to stay close to her.

"I'm guessing there's not going to be any more gift baskets from you," she said with a wry smile.

"Who knows," he said.

"Well, there's nothing left from our days together," she said.

"You're right. I've found that my grand scheme for revenge wasn't what I thought it would be."

"Do you forgive me?" she asked.

Did he? When he'd first arrived in Orlando he would have said that nothing short of making her dependent on him and then leaving her would have quenched his need for revenge. But now? Forgiveness, it was something odd. His mom always said in order to forgive someone you have to acknowledge they hurt you. And Mitch still wasn't ready to admit he could be hurt.

"You know how I told you about my family's tradition of falling in love?"

"Yes."

Confession was supposed to be good for the soul.

Knowing he'd never see her again, he needed to bring some sort of closure to the past. "Well, I did think you were the one. And I realize now how little I knew about you. How little I let you see about me."

"So you think it was just lust?" she asked. He knew she was hurt. Just lust. It was hard to label what they'd had then or now. They were like dry timber and a flame. They couldn't coexist happily for too long, but while the flames were burning bright it felt so good, so right.

"I'm not sure. I do know that you weren't only to blame for what happened. A part of me was so hungry to prove myself I'd take any risk."

"I don't agree. I definitely set you up to take the fall."

"Yes, you did. But I let you."

"I set you up with the partners."

"I know."

"I don't blame you for wanting revenge."

"I do. I could've stayed and fought back. I chose to leave."

"Like now," she said. Stepping back into her house she closed the door quietly. He stood there for a moment. And then turned on his heel and walked away. He had work to do when he got back to L.A.

He started running through the week in his head but all he saw was Sophia's eyes watching him.

SOPHIA GOT OFF THE PLANE in LAX with no clear plan in mind. She only knew that she'd driven Mitch away once long ago and the last five days without him had been too long and too lonely. Maybe she was having a midlife crisis, though she knew in her heart she wasn't.

For the first time ever she'd decided to follow her heart and nothing was scaring her more. The airport was teeming with people and she'd never felt more alone. This was a mistake. What in the world was she going to say to Mitch? She didn't even know where he lived or if he'd welcome her.

Indecision was foreign to her and she forced it firmly out of her mind. Of course Mitch would welcome her. He hadn't wanted to leave her in Orlando. She knew it and he knew it.

She collected her luggage. A group of Asian tourists swarmed around her and for a minute she felt like she was in a foreign land. Taking her suitcase, she worked her way through the crowd, found a quiet bench to sit down, and turned on her cell phone.

She called information and got the number to Mitch's firm. What should she say? She'd be cool and see what he said. Let him make the first move, she told herself firmly.

She dialed the number and waited to be connected to his office. She hadn't felt this…indecisive since she'd made the decision to send Mitch out of their apartment ten years ago.

"Hollaran," he said.

She almost dropped the phone. God, what if he didn't want her anymore?

"Is anyone there?" he asked. He sounded impatient.

"It's me," she said.

"Sophia? What can I do for you?" he asked. She knew he had to be busy after spending so much time on the East Coast for the Spinder case. This was probably the worst time to call him.

She took a deep breath. *Be cool.* "I'm on vacation for one more week. Can I come and stay with you?"

"Ah…why?"

In for a penny, in for a pound, she thought. This trip wasn't as impulsive as she'd thought when she'd driven to the airport this morning. This was a trip she should've taken ten years ago. Mitch Hollaran and she had unfinished business. And living on separate coasts wasn't going to change the fact that they still hadn't found closure.

"Sophia?"

"I miss you."

He said nothing. She heard his chair creak and imagined him lounging back, feet on his desk. She'd given up all the power she'd acquired in the last ten years. She'd given up everything she'd worked for her entire life. She'd taken a huge risk and it had backfired.

"I guess that answers my question."

"No, it doesn't," he said.

"I know we said no strings."

"We did say no strings, so is this just a continuation of our weekend, Sophia? Or do you want something more?"

"I don't know. My town house was too quiet and I thought maybe spending the rest of my time off with you would be nice."

"Nice?"

"Nice," she said. Actually it would be a hell of a lot better than nice but she'd been afraid to risk her heart. Even though he held the key to her future she knew she still didn't want to let him know.

"Well, I'll have to think about it."

She didn't handle anxiety well so instead of being cool like she'd wanted to, she snapped, "What's there to think about?"

"I have to work. You distract me."

"You did fine in Orlando."

"That was different."

"How?" she asked. It was almost as if he were

saying she was more important to him than he'd let on before.

"I was still working under the revenge premise. It was easier to justify thinking about you."

"And now you're afraid you can't," she said, quietly.

"I'm not afraid of anything, Sophia Marie."

"Glad one of us isn't."

"Where are you?" he asked at last.

No way was she telling him. He didn't even want her to visit him. "You don't want to know."

"Yes, I do."

She let the silence build on the line for a few long minutes before she finally sighed and said, "I'm at the airport."

"Orlando's?"

"No." She wasn't going to say any more. She'd thought he'd given up on revenge but there was something in his tone and his reluctance to see her again that made her doubt that belief.

"You're in Los Angeles, aren't you." It was a statement and not a question.

"I am."

"Babe…"

"I know. Take your revenge if that's what you want, Mitch. Tell me to go home, and then savor the feeling. I promise you it doesn't last for long."

He sighed. "I already know that."

"You do?"

"Every time I think I've beaten you, I end up feeling an ache deep inside."

"I didn't mean to make this worse."

"You didn't."

"What hotel are you staying at? I'll meet you there after work."

"I didn't make a reservation."

He sighed.

She wished she'd never gotten on the plane and left Florida.

"Got a pen?" he asked at last.

"Yes," she said, digging a notepad and pen from her purse.

"Here's my home address."

She jotted it down.

"Got it?"

"Yes."

"Good. I'll call my housekeeper and tell her to expect you."

"I shouldn't have come," she said at last.

"Maybe. But I'm glad you did."

"You weren't sure you wanted me here."

"Hell, woman, I've always wanted you here."

"Then what's the problem?" she asked. She'd never felt so vulnerable in her entire life.

"I'm trying to decide if seeing you is worth the pain of watching you leave again."

Her stomach dropped. He hung up before she could respond. She wasn't the only one who needed closure, she realized. Mitch still didn't trust her. That was okay, she didn't trust herself. She only knew that she needed more time with Mitch before she took the Deputy District Attorney's job and gave up on a personal life.

MITCH STAYED LATE AT WORK, not leaving until after seven. The traffic on the 5 was heavy, but still he made it home in forty-five minutes. He parked his car in the circle drive and sat there.

Sophia was in his home.

It was a sobering thought. A part of him wanted to send his house staff home, lock the gates and never let her leave. But he knew he couldn't.

Another part...the young man who'd been betrayed in Cambridge ten years earlier, wanted to put the car back in gear and drive away before she hurt him again.

But he'd never been a coward. If Dev could face his worst fears and come back a stronger man, so could Mitch. Dev had gone to Julie's, and while not being pleased with the lies Dev had told her, Julie had given him a second chance.

Mitch wasn't interested in second chances. He wasn't interested in do-overs or anything that meant the past had to be repeated. He wanted to keep everything with Sophia fresh and new.

He pocketed his keys, grabbed his briefcase and climbed out of the car. The house was quiet when he entered it. He stopped by his study and dropped off his briefcase and checked his voice mail. There was a message from Dev. Mitch knew Dev was just checking in and not seeking a problem solver. Their relationship had changed in the last few weeks.

Dev was realizing that despite Mitch's outward appearance he didn't lead a charmed life all the time. Okay, he was delaying. He knew when he saw her again he was going to want things that he shouldn't, that those dreams he'd been trying to once again forget were going to seem sharper and more real.

Loosening his tie, he stepped out onto the deck, went to the railing and looked out over his backyard.

He felt someone else's presence on the deck with him. The ripple down his spine told him it was Sophia. This was what he'd been afraid of when she'd said she was at LAX.

His body still craved her like a sweet addiction. He knew that his soul still hungered for her because he woke up every night in a tangle of twisted sheets calling out her name. His heart, that battered organ, still ached for something he wasn't sure he could find with Sophia.

He heard her footsteps on the wooden deck as she

moved toward him. The soft rustle of bare feet against hardwood. In his mind he saw her as she'd been on the balcony in Boca wearing nothing but that colorful scarf he'd packed for her.

He tensed. Not knowing why, yet at the same time he did know why. This was the one thing he'd lusted after. *Sophia Deltonio in his home.* Now that she was here, what was he going to do with her? He didn't think he could let her go again. He'd been questioning himself since he left Orlando.

"Evening," she said, stopping next to him.

She smelled good. Light and floral—fresh and exciting. Glancing to his left, he saw she wore a pair of khaki shorts and a plain T-shirt. Her thick hair was caught back in a ponytail and that velvet ribbon was around her neck. She certainly hadn't dressed to entice him.

But she did all the same.

There was some indefinable emotion in her eyes as she stood quietly next to him. Was he seeing what he wanted to see? He'd realized something over the past few days they'd been apart. Sophia wasn't going to ever be completely out of his soul. It didn't matter what kind of revenge he took on her or didn't take. She would always be a part of the fabric of his being.

"Where's Maria?" he asked to distract himself from those lips of hers which were too enticing.

Sophia shrugged and tipped her head to the side. "I'm not used to having a housekeeper around. When you called to say you were coming home late, I sent her home."

They were alone. If he wanted to, he could pull her into his arms and make love to her on the deck. He knew she wouldn't turn him away. Sophia never did when it came to the physical. But he needed more than soul sex. He needed soul mating. Not just bodies but souls, and he didn't know if Sophia was willing to give him her soul.

"Did you eat dinner yet?" he asked.

She shook her head and moved a little closer to him. "I'm not hungry for food."

"Why are you here?" he asked abruptly. Yeah, you could tell he was one of the most eloquent lawyers in California.

She nibbled her lower lip. He knew she didn't mean for the action to be sexual but it was. Everything she did became an enticement to him. "I don't know for sure."

"I thought you missed me."

"I did."

"Isn't that why you came?" he asked, silkily.

"It is and it isn't."

"Are we really going to play games?"

"Why shouldn't we? We're both good at them."

"Maybe I'm tired of playing."

"Oh... I'll get my things and call a cab."

"I didn't ask you to leave."

"What do you want from me?"

"I'd settle for some honesty."

She swallowed and pivoted to face the backyard again. "I...I missed you and I wanted to see if we could have more than just an affair between us."

That was exactly what he was afraid of because he knew they had the potential to be more than lovers. And he wasn't sure he'd be able to really trust her with his heart a second time.

16

SOPHIA HAD NEVER FELT SO vulnerable as she did as the silence between her and Mitch lengthened. She had nothing left to lose. Coming to L.A. had stripped her bare. And she'd realized as she'd stood there in the teeming crowds that she hadn't come to Los Angeles for a vacation. She wanted to stay in Mitch's house and his life for the rest of her life.

When she'd arrived in Bel Air at his home, another piece of the puzzle that was Mitch had fallen into place. This house wasn't just a place to crash at the end of the day. The backyard was a lush tropically landscaped area, but the pool was a child's delight. Mitch's house was a place to bring a family to. As soon as she'd looked through the sprawling mansion she'd realized part of the reason why he'd decided to seek revenge against her in the first place.

Mitch wanted a family but he hadn't been able to move on. She knew this because she'd been stuck in the same kind of limbo until their weekend. That wasn't true, she realized suddenly. She'd started changing before they'd even met face-to-face again.

As soon as that Corona tub had appeared on her desk she'd started falling for him again.

She only hoped she could do as good a job convincing him that they needed a second chance as she did in the courtroom. Because she knew that she wasn't going to ever find another man like Mitch. Hell, the last ten years had proven that he was the only man for her.

He still hadn't said anything. She cleared her throat and tried to think of something to say.

"Um…your mom called after Maria left. She thought I was one of your new maids."

"Did you tell her you weren't?" he asked.

"No," she said. His mom had sounded really nice on the phone. Her speech patterns were similar to Mitch's. Sophia had almost confessed who she really was but the thought of telling his mom that she was the reason Mitch had left Harvard all those years ago had stopped her.

"Why not?" he asked. He turned to face her. He still wore his suit. Another one of those powerful dark ones he wore all the time. He'd shed his tie and jacket. His collar was open.

"I figured if your mom knew who I was she'd probably not like me very much."

She wondered what he'd do if she just said to hell with this conversation that was making her regret ever getting on the plane. They communicated so much better on the physical level. "My family doesn't hate you."

She didn't want to talk about his family. She wanted him to tell her how he felt about her so she could feel safe revealing to him all the feelings she'd bottled up for too long. "They can't like me very much. I'm the reason you didn't graduate from Harvard."

Mitch shrugged and looked away from her. "My dad owns a hardware store. They didn't care about Harvard."

"Yes, but still. I was the woman who betrayed you." Just saying the words made her ache deep inside. Her family knew about Mitch. She'd told her mom about him the summer after graduation when it was clear that he was never coming back. When it was clear that he'd never really wanted her more than he'd wanted an intern position at a prestigious law firm. Her mother had been disappointed in her for not putting her heart in front of her head. But in the end Sophia had felt she'd made the right decision. Until this moment.

Until she realized she'd hurt Mitch and probably hurt his family's dreams for him.

Abruptly he turned away from her. "I never told them about you."

Shock rippled through her. She certainly didn't want to be disliked by his family but she'd expected something different. But she shouldn't have. She knew that once she stepped outside the courtroom, life got sticky. That's why she'd decided that her job would be the sole focus of her life.

"What? I thought you said you were going to ask me to marry you."

He shoved his hands deep into his pockets. Something she realized he did when he was agitated. He'd done it a couple of times in court. "I was."

"But you never mentioned me to your family? Where's the trust now, Mitch?" she asked. Never before had she felt like a bigger idiot. God, why hadn't she realized that Mitch would never trust her? He couldn't because he'd made up his mind about her long ago. And nothing, not even the weekend they'd spent in Boca—the one that had changed her perspective—was going to change his mind about her.

"I have issues with looking like a fool."

She crossed her arms over her chest and took a few steps away from him. "Everyone does."

"Not like me. Want a drink?" he asked, crossing to the minibar. He pulled out two Coronas and set them on the bar.

She shook her head. She needed her wits about her when she was talking to Mitch. She'd envisioned their reunion in one of two ways. Either red-hot spent entirely in bed or a very brief polite exchange of words. But this was different.

Of course he'd have Coronas. He probably had Stevie in the CD player. She tried to take some reassurance from that. They weren't really all that different. The things that affected her deeply affected him as well.

"No. I think I better leave. The reasons why I came here—well, that doesn't matter any more."

"Why *did* you come here?"

"I came here looking for something that doesn't exist."

"What?"

"Don't make me say it. I think I've looked stupid enough for one day, showing up like I did without calling first."

"I didn't think that was stupid."

"No, it probably was a big ego stroke for you. Despite what you might think given my recent behavior, I do have some ego left and I'd like to take those shreds with me when I go home. Goodbye, Mitch. I hope you find the family you need to fill this house with love."

She walked into his house and out of his life, hoping she could make it to the foyer and her bags before the tears that burned the back of her eyes started to fall.

REVENGE WAS a bitterly cold place and Mitch knew if he let Sophia walk out his front door he'd have it in spades, but he'd known from the moment he'd walked in his front door that it was the last thing on his mind. He'd had a hard time sleeping since he'd returned to the West Coast. And he could blame it on jet lag and his caseload, but the truth was he slept better when Sophia was in bed with him.

He grabbed her arm before she could take another step. She felt small and fragile under his big hand. He knew she was formidable. But he always forgot that was an image she projected and not her physical form.

Letting her go wasn't an option. Seeing her here in the home he'd created, he realized he'd built this house for her. *For them.* For the family he'd always imagined them having. He now knew in his heart that for her to trust him, he had to first trust her.

"Don't go," he said. Suddenly power and control didn't matter. If he were alone—if he let her leave him then he wouldn't have any power at all. He'd be a broken man again and he didn't want to go back there.

"I can't do this now—not tonight. Let me go to a hotel and I'll call you in the morning," she said. Her voice was low and husky filled with emotions that he knew she didn't want to reveal, and he knew because he'd been hiding his feelings for a long time.

She wasn't staying anywhere but here in his house. In his king-size bed upstairs. He tugged her back against him, burying his face in her neck. God, she smelled sweet and sensual. He knew if he touched her, he could elicit a physical reaction that would postpone this conversation.

He turned his head and started to brush her hair aside but stopped at the last second. They didn't need to make love now. They needed to talk and clear the air in a way they never had. And she'd been right when she'd asked about honesty. It was well past time that he confessed how deeply she'd been embedded into his heart and soul.

He didn't want to face her. Didn't want her to see what her walking away from him had done to him.

"This isn't about ego," he said at last.

"Then what is it about?" she whispered.

Her hands rested on his arms where he held her. He glanced over her shoulder down at their bodies. She looked so right in his arms. Felt so damned right there that he decided to do whatever it took to keep her here.

He remembered the first night he'd walked back into her life and what he'd said as they'd shared a cocktail in the lounge. He'd said he wanted to exorcise her from his dreams. But he'd only just realized that he didn't have any dreams that didn't involve her. And if he exorcised her from them he'd have nothing but a cold and lonely future.

"It's about—dammit, woman—I'm not sure how to say this."

She turned in his embrace, her hands cupping his face as she rose on tiptoe to brush her lips against his. "Mitch, I came here because I don't want to spend the rest of my life without you."

Words deserted him. She'd taken a risk he was still afraid to take. Sophia Deltonio—the woman he'd always thought of as cool and unemotional—had shown him that she was still the bravest person he'd ever met.

"Oh, God, woman…me too." He peppered kisses over her face and then finally took her mouth.

"Really?"

"Really. I love you, Sophia. I didn't want to. I tried to pretend revenge was the only thing I wanted from you—you know, a chance to win back my pride. But deep inside I knew the truth."

"What truth?" she asked. Her hands on his face were cool and he closed his eyes for a moment and just let himself savor the feelings that were rushing through him.

"That I wanted you back in my arms. Everything I've achieved in my professional career was to impress you. To show you I was the guy you needed by your side.''

''Mitch—''

He covered her mouth with two fingers. He had more to say. And he never wanted to have to say any of these things again. ''Don't say anything. Let me finish.

''I built this house because I want a family. And I dated some nice women and brought them here but they didn't fit in. Nothing felt right.

''Until you.''

He got down on one knee. ''I want you to marry me.''

He pulled the ring he'd purchased ten years ago out of his pocket.

''Did you buy this ring when you built the house?'' she asked.

He shook his head. ''I bought it in Cambridge right before spring break.''

She started to cry and sank down next to him on the floor. He wrapped his arms around her and held her tightly to him. He was painfully aware that she hadn't said she'd be his wife. Or that she loved him. Feeling like a bigger fool than he'd ever have thought possible, he comforted the only woman to ever own his heart.

''I don't deserve you,'' she said.

''Why not?'' he asked.

"What kind of woman doesn't know the man she loves is about to propose to her? What kind of woman betrays that man and then never contacts him again? What kind of woman—"

He stopped her with his lips. She tasted of tears and something that he associated only with Sophia. He lifted his head after long minutes. "The only kind of woman for me."

"I love you, Mitch," she said.

He stood and lifted her into his arms and carried her out into the Eden that was his backyard. He wanted to make love to Sophia, and to seal their commitment in front of nature and the universe.

He slipped the ring on her finger and she kissed him as he carried her down the steps toward the pool.

MITCH MADE LOVE TO HER with no preliminaries, just a straightforward claiming of his mate. He stripped them both bare and laid her on a padded chaise lounge then put her feet on his shoulders and entered with one long thrust.

"You're mine."

"Yes," she said.

He held her hips with his strong hands and her eyes with his mesmerizing gaze. She shuddered under the impact of his thrusts and they both came together.

He cradled her in his arms afterward using his body heat to keep them both warm on the balmy summer night. The flowers filled the air with a natural fragrance and the night had a dreamlike quality to it.

Sophia didn't want to end that magic but she was practical and her mind was buzzing with questions.

"Where will we live?" Sophia asked abruptly.

Mitch stopped stroking her back. "That's up to you. You have a big job waiting for you in Orlando. Are you going to take it?"

"I haven't thought of anything but you since I've been on vacation," she admitted.

"That's not the Sophia I know." He started caressing her back again with broad strokes of his hand.

"But it is," she said, softly. Turning in his arms, she touched his face, framing his beard-stubbled cheeks. "I only focused on my career because I was afraid to let my heart rule. But that's no longer the case."

"What are you saying, counselor?" he asked, more serious than she'd ever seen him before. She'd realized earlier that loving her made Mitch vulnerable and she was still coming to terms with the fact that this very self-assured man could have a weakness.

"That I think I want to live here in this house

you built for our family. I'll have to take the bar in California and find a job.''

"Sounds great to me. You don't have to work if you don't want to.''

She thought about that for a minute. Not practice law—no way. "I have to. It's a big part of who I am.''

"I'm fine with whatever decision you make. But I do have one request.''

"And that is…''

He caressed the thin black ribbon around her neck. "Wear this at home.''

She nodded. He caressed her neck and shivers spread throughout her body. She knew it represented the same thing to Mitch as it did to her. A connection to that first love they'd shared, but hadn't been able to control.

He lowered his head and kissed her neck where the ribbon was, tracing his tongue between her skin and the fabric.

She wanted to make love to her man but she had one more concern. "What about your family?'' she asked.

"Sophia, they'll love you. My mom's been after me to settle down forever.''

"But I'm the reason you didn't for so long.''

"Babe, we're working on a legend here.''

"What kind of legend?''

"The ballad of Sophia and Mitch…star-crossed lovers, stubborn lawyers who had to wait ten years to realize they were meant to be together. If there's one thing my parents love it's a romantic legend."

Sophia's heart felt as if it could burst with love for this man. She pushed him onto his back and made love to him slowly. Kissing and caressing every inch of his body. Offering him her breasts and letting him suckle her. Then she mounted him and took him into her body. Their building toward climax this time was slow and leisurely and finally it broke over them at the same time.

She sank down on Mitch and closed her eyes knowing she'd found the one thing she'd always wanted. A man who could tame the restlessness inside her.

"Revenge is sweet," Mitch said against her hair.

"Really?"

"It got me you, didn't it?"

"I guess it did."

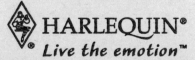

**The Queen of Sizzle
brings you sheer steamy
reading at its best!**

USA TODAY
Bestselling Author

LORI
FOSTER

FALLEN
ANGELS

**Two full-length novels
plus a brand-new novella!**

The three women in these
stories are no angels...
and neither are
the men they love!

Available February 2004.

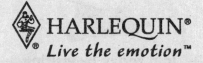

HARLEQUIN®
Live the emotion™

Visit us at www.eHarlequin.com

PHFA

HARLEQUIN®

Temptation

THE WRONG BED

What happens when a girl finds herself in the
wrong bed...with the *right* guy?

Find out in:

#866 NAUGHTY BY NATURE by Jule McBride
February 2002

#870 SOMETHING WILD by Toni Blake
March 2002

#874 CARRIED AWAY by Donna Kauffman
April 2002

#878 HER PERFECT STRANGER by Jill Shalvis
May 2002

#882 BARELY MISTAKEN by Jennifer LaBrecque
June 2002

#886 TWO TO TANGLE by Leslie Kelly
July 2002

Midnight mix-ups have never been so much fun!

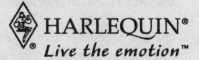